YA Peyman
Peymani, Christine
Chasing mavericks : the movie
novelization /

34028082624629
BC $8.99   ocn803946333
04/10/13

CHASING MAVERICKS

THE MOVIE NOVELIZATION

STORY BY JIM MEENAGHAN &
BRANDON HOOPER

SCREENPLAY BY KARIO SALEM
AND BRANDON HOOPER

ADAPTATION BY CHRISTINE PEYMANI

HARPER
An Imprint of HarperCollinsPublishers

Chasing Mavericks: The Movie Novelization

Copyright © 2012 Twentieth Century Fox Film Corporation and Walden Media, LLC
All rights reserved. Printed in the United States of America. No part of this book may
be used or reproduced in any manner whatsoever without written permission except in
the case of brief quotations embodied in critical articles and reviews. For information
address HarperCollins Children's Books, a division of HarperCollins Publishers,
10 East 53rd Street, New York, NY 10022.
www.epicreads.com

Library of Congress Cataloging-in-Publication Data is available.
ISBN 978-0-06-220042-6

Typography by Tom Starace
12 13 14 15 16 LP/RRDH   10 9 8 7 6 5 4 3 2 1
❖
First Edition

CHASING MAVERICKS

PROLOGUE

Far beneath the waves that had carried him so many times before, he drifted down, down. At this depth, the light barely filtering onto his chiseled face, he felt weightless, limitless, unafraid. This was the ocean, his ocean, and if it was his time to submit to it after years of conquering its turbulence—well, this was not the worst fate he could imagine.

His arms drifted at his sides, and he whispered, "Sixty"—or not even a whisper, just the slightest movement of his lips as he folded his third finger, leaving only his thumb and index finger, pointed like a gun. This was the way to keep track of time in the abyss. You run out of fingers, you're out of time. He was almost out of both. He began to rise from the ocean floor, his breathing slow and steady, knowing he had pushed the limits far enough. But then he seemed to freeze, somewhere between the depths and the surface.

He thought he could make out a voice coming from somewhere, though down here all was silent. "We all come from the sea, but we are not all of the sea. Those of us who are, we children of the tides, must return to it, again and again."

He recognized the voice now. It was his mentor,

the only one who had always been at his side when he faced the ocean. The two of them were men of the sea. Return to it—that was all he was doing now. No need to fight, no need to fear. And then he felt himself floating up, up, high above the shimmering surface of the tropical waters.

The voice seemed to speak to him again: "There exists a strange freedom, which isn't possible on land. A detachment from the human world, where time and turmoil become nothing more than an afterthought."

Now the ocean began to churn as lightning flashed and thunder clapped. Ships and freighters tossed like toys on the violent swells. Below, all was peaceful still, but he felt the sea's power surging around him. Somehow he was both above and below the water now, but overtaken with the calm his mentor had spoken of so many times. He'd always heard about people's lives flashing before their eyes. It had even happened to him, once before, years ago, also beneath the ocean. Now the memories came flooding in—not of his whole life, but of the parts that mattered most: his life with her and his life on the sea.

CHAPTER 1

◀ ▶

1986

Crash! The wave smashed into the white cliffs of Santa Cruz. Jay Moriarity shouted in excitement as an icy spray spattered him where he stood on a stone shelf halfway down the cliff's face. Beside him stood his best friend, Kim Ward Williams, huddled against the cold he barely felt himself. Wrapping her bright blue jacket tighter around her shoulders, she held a tennis ball in one hand and a squirming brown-and-white puppy in her arms.

"One thousand one, one thousand two . . ." Jay chanted to himself, not flinching at the thunderous crash of the wave against the cliff, or the chill of the water against his cheeks.

"C'mon, Jay, let's go!" Kim shouted over the sound of the tide. Her wispy white-blond hair whirled around her face in the strong winds off the ocean. "We're gonna get wet!" She set her puppy down and began the steep climb back to the top of the cliff. He didn't seem to hear her, his focus locked on the next approaching wave. "Come on, Sophie," Kim called to her dog. The puppy scurried after her, large paws scrambling for traction in the scrubby brush that dotted the cliff side.

The wave slammed against the cliff, loud as thunder. "You see that?" Jay exclaimed. "It's building! That was the longest yet." A fine spray from the froth below spattered his face and scalp beneath his military-style crew cut. Now he shivered, but he didn't back away.

Kim was already struggling up the rock face, her blue skirt tangling around her legs. As she leaned down to tug it free, the tennis ball slipped from her fingers. It bounced into the waxy leaves of an ice plant, one of many that sprouted from between the rocks. After balancing on the pointy tips for a moment, the ball slid off, down the rocky tiers of the cliff. Sophie launched herself eagerly after it, bounding toward the waves crashing below.

"Sophie, no!" Kim cried. She grabbed for the puppy's brand-new green collar, but grasped only air.

Jay spun to see the tiny brown-and-white blur scampering downward. He took in the ball rolling across the reef and the wave looming toward the shore. Without a second thought, he leapt down, charging across the reef to grab the tennis ball. Snatching it from the rocks, he heaved it up toward an ice plant above him. Sophie's feet skittered on the rocks as she executed a midair U-turn to continue the chase.

Jay smiled, relieved to see that the dog was safe. But as he turned, he realized that he was not. A solid wall of black water loomed toward him menacingly as he raced back across the reef.

"Jay, no, look out!" Kim shouted, knowing her words wouldn't reach him over the deafening noise of the wave—and even if he heard her, he would never be able to outrun the wave. Suddenly, he vanished beneath the crush of water.

"Help! Somebody, please, help!" Kim screamed, clutching her puppy to her chest as she desperately searched the water below for some sign of her friend, looking to the cliff above for some sign of help. But they were alone out here—and now she was alone, completely.

Far below, Jay fought the undertow that sucked him under, the frigid current that dragged him out to sea. He spun in the swirling turbulence with no way of telling which direction was up or down, shore or sea. His breath had been snatched from him, and he felt himself teetering on the edge of blackout as he struggled to keep from inhaling the water instead.

But just when he thought all hope was gone, a massive hand grasped him and yanked him from the ocean's clutches. As his head broke the surface, he sucked in air in a heaving gasp, shaking water from his short brown hair and blinking it from his blue eyes.

His rescuer shoved Jay onto the front of his longboard as the biggest wave yet rose before them. Jay caught a glimpse of the man's graying waves of dark-blond hair with a goatee to match, framing a weathered face grim with concentration.

The man paddled hard away from the wave, arm muscles bulging, but the wave was already starting to crest. "Hang on!" he shouted, before pivoting his longboard and paddling into the wave instead.

Jay clutched the board, his eyes wide, feeling the rush as the board rose with the surge of the wave. Suddenly, he was face-to-face with a sheer wall of water, and time seemed to stop as they balanced at its peak. Then the surfer slipped to his knees, bracing Jay as they shot down the wave. Jay knew he should have been terrified, but he was too caught up in the thrill to feel any fear.

Plenty of times, he had admired the Santa Cruz surfers while he timed the waves from above. But, somehow, it had never occurred to him that he could join them. Now, with the wind rushing in his ears, the salt spray spattering his face, the feeling of oneness with the entire massive ocean that surrounded him—he knew it wasn't just something he wanted to do, it was something he *had* to do. In that moment, he became certain that surfing was his destiny.

When the wave released them to the shore, he was so overcome with excitement that he forgot to even thank his rescuer. "Wow!" he exclaimed instead. "That was amazing! How did you learn—"

But the man stopped him. "That was lucky, is

what that was. You could've died out there, just as easy."

His enthusiasm immediately dampened, Jay looked down at his hands. "Yeah, I know, I—I was just helping my friend, and . . ." He didn't really know how to explain. It seemed ridiculous to have risked his life for a dog, yet, he couldn't imagine having done anything less. He couldn't have just stood by while that helpless puppy was swept away. Besides, Kim was crazy about that dog, and Jay would have done anything for her.

Before he had to say anything more, Kim rushed over to them and threw her arms around Jay, Sophie jumping at her legs. "Are you okay? I can't believe you're okay!" She held him at arm's length, looking him up and down as though examining him for damage. "When I saw you go under, I thought . . . I mean, I didn't see anyone, and then suddenly . . ."

She turned to the older man, her eyes shining with gratitude and admiration, but he just gruffly muttered, "Well, come on then." He pivoted and led the way up to steps to the top of the cliff, where their bikes and his van waited. Scrambling to keep up with his determined march, Kim and Jay exchanged glances but didn't say a word.

As they started to grab their bikes, the man shook his head. "Might as well get you home, make sure you don't ride your bikes into oncoming traffic." He yanked open the rear doors of his white van, revealing a scattered pile of construction tools. Picking up both bikes at once like they were toys, he slung them into the back, where they clattered against the tools. While Sophie bounded around their feet, he peeled off his dripping wetsuit and slung it in, too. In his board shorts, and with his broad, heavily muscled chest revealed, the man looked even more like a surf god. Tossing Jay a towel, he motioned them into the backseat.

Wrapped in the towel and beaming with pure excitement, Jay clambered into the back. Kim hesitated for a moment, and Jay knew she was thinking of all the warnings they had ever gotten to never get into a car with a stranger. But this man was a hero, and Jay trusted him completely. As he nodded to Kim, he saw her reach the same conclusion. Clutching Sophie close, she climbed in behind him, zipping the puppy inside her jacket for warmth. Jay's gray sweatshirt and jeans were so heavy with water that he felt plastered to the seat, and he soon gave up even trying to dry them with the already soggy towel.

"Thank you so much, Mister—" Kim began as the man slid into the driver's seat, but he cut her off.

"It's Frosty. Just Frosty." Irritation and relief warred for control of his features. Then he caught a glimpse of Jay's huge grin in the rearview mirror, and he settled on a glare.

"Oh, you're smiling now, big shot. But if I hadn't paddled around the point at that exact moment . . ." He let his words trail off. They all knew how incredibly lucky Jay had been. "How old are you anyway? Six? Seven?"

"Eight and three-quarters, sir," Jay replied, sitting up as tall and straight as he could.

"Well, you just used up your entire lifetime allotment of dumb luck. Keep that in mind the next time you and your sister decide to play on the cliffs at high tide." With that, Frosty snapped on his radio, the Grateful Dead's "Sugar Magnolia" blasting through the vehicle.

Jay's gaze roved over every inch of the van, taking in the maps and charts tucked behind the seat, the dog-eared copies of Jack London's *The Sea Wolf* and Thoreau's *Walden*. He wanted to examine every one, read through every page, absorb every bit of information he could about the ocean, especially if any of it would help him become even a little more like the man who had just saved his life.

Kim's voice cut through his thoughts. "By the way, I'm not his sister. And *I'm* ten and a half."

Frosty clicked the music off, letting the silence descend uncomfortably before he finally replied. "Well, there you go. It's making more sense by the minute. An *older* woman, no less. So here's a novel idea: On your next little date, why don't you go to the arcade, or peewee golfing. Something that doesn't involve you getting killed."

Jay wanted to point out that it wasn't a date, but Kim went right on talking before he could say anything.

"Because he likes to time the waves," she announced. Jay elbowed her, trying to shush her, but she didn't care. "What? You do."

"Whaddya mean, *time* the waves?" Frosty was glaring at them in the rearview mirror again.

Jay shifted uncomfortably in his seat, sure this was just going to annoy Frosty more.

"Ever since they moved here from South Carolina—I mean, Jay and his mom." Kim leaned forward in her seat, apparently ready to spill her friend's life story. "His dad's in the Special Forces and until—"

"Whoa, whoa, whoa," Frosty interrupted her. "Boy's got a tongue." He turned to shoot Jay a look. "Why do you time the waves? And give me the *Reader's Digest* version."

"Um . . . to see if the swell is building or dropping." His eyes were lowered with embarrassment at first, but he quickly warmed to his topic, his voice growing steadier as he met Frosty's gaze. "The more seconds between them—you know, each wave in a set—means it's getting bigger."

"Who taught you that?" Frosty demanded, and Jay dropped his eyes again. Somehow he just kept getting on this man's nerves.

Jay looked from Kim to Frosty before admitting, "Nobody, sir. Just figured it out."

"That's the Boussinesq approximation. You just figured that out on your own?" Frosty didn't sound annoyed anymore. He sounded impressed.

Jay nodded self-consciously as they locked eyes in the rearview mirror. But he could manage only a moment under the intensity of Frosty's stare. Turning away, he gazed out at the lights of the Santa Cruz wharf and boardwalk glittering in the distance, jutting out over the dark ocean.

Besides muttering directions to his house, Jay didn't speak for the rest of the drive. Frosty seemed content to remain silent, too, though Jay caught Kim shooting him looks he knew were meant to encourage him to talk. He didn't know why he was so intimidated by this man, except that Frosty was the best surfer he had ever met and, of course, the fact that he was literally Jay's hero. Probably that was plenty.

When they pulled up in front of the weathered bungalow that Jay shared with his mom, he and Kim hopped out to unload their bikes. He felt Frosty's eyes on them and tried not to behave differently because of it. Would he normally have pulled the bike out so fast, or been so careful in standing it up once he did? He couldn't be sure. Slamming the van's rear door shut, he drew a deep breath and circled to the driver's side door.

He rapped on the window until Frosty, with a sigh, rolled it down. "What now?"

"Just wanted to say thank you." Jay could barely meet the older man's eyes, but he forced himself to look up at him.

"You're welcome." Frosty stared right back at him, hands clenched on the steering wheel, obviously ready to be gone. "So, why're you still standing there?"

"Um . . ." Jay felt tongue-tied in a way he never had before. He knew he had wanted to say something important, but now it seemed out of reach. "How big you reckon that wave was, sir?" That was one of the many things he wanted to ask—not the most important question, but better than nothing.

"It's a small world, kid, but how they gauge the size of waves differs from place to place. So, hard to say." Frosty eased the van forward, apparently finished with this conversation, but Jay wasn't willing to let him go.

He trotted alongside the van, gaining confidence—or maybe just desperation—now that Frosty was almost gone. "So it might be bigger somewhere else?"

Frosty hit the brakes, heaving a bigger sigh this time, but giving in to Jay's persistence anyway.

"In the islands, for example, where the sport of kings originated, surfers measure waves by their backside," he explained. Jay nodded, wide-eyed, soaking up the information. "Which, of course, is contrary to North America, where we measure 'em tip to trough. Regardless, it was definitely *big enough*. Okay?"

With that, Frosty sped off down the narrow one-way street, before turning into a driveway less than a block away. When Frosty climbed out, he looked at Jay standing only a few houses away from his and shook his head. "Like I said—small world, kid."

Then he disappeared through his front gate, while Jay still stood frozen in the road behind him. All this time, he had been living less than a block from a surfing god, and he'd had no idea. It had to be fate.

When Kim joined him a moment later, he was still staring at Frosty's place, hoping to catch another glimpse of his rescuer.

"Appreciate you saving Sophie, Jay," she said. "One of the bravest things I've ever seen." Kim leaned in and gave him a quick peck on the cheek before racing off down the street, grabbing her bike and leaping aboard. Jay stood there shocked once more, his cheeks hot as he broke into a huge grin. It had been a day full of surprises, but that kiss from his best friend might have been the most surprising thing of all.

Still smiling, he walked into the little

ramshackle house and flicked on a light. He glanced at the tiny kitchen, where their tenant's parrot perched in her cage on the counter, then toward the old blue bedsheet hanging in the corner, cordoning off his makeshift bedroom. He yanked off his wet jacket and laid it on the kitchen counter beside a torn-open envelope. A cashier's check sat atop it, and he picked it up. It was made out for four hundred dollars, pay to the order of Christy Moriarity—his mom. From the account of Sergeant D. Moriarity, US Army. That would be his absent father. As he laid it back down, he noticed a crumpled letter lying on the threadbare gray carpet.

He read it quickly, face twitching to hold back the tears as waves of hurt, anger, and confusion swept over him. But he fought off his feelings, refusing to cry, and headed down the short hallway to find his mother.

"Mom?" he called, his voice cracking on the single word.

Peeking into her bedroom, he saw her sprawled across her bed. He crept into the room, pausing to sniff a carton of orange juice that sat open on her nightstand. Its rancid smell burned his nostrils, and he wrinkled his nose in disgust.

His mom's eyes fluttered open and she peered at him blearily, as though trying to bring him into focus. She looked worn-out, older than her thirty-five years, her blond hair tangled and her face red and gaunt. But she was still his mother, and he still thought she was beautiful.

"Sorry, baby," she muttered, voice slurred with sleep. "Mommy ain't feeling so good today."

"Don't worry," he said, trying to be strong for her. "Dad'll change his mind."

She met his gaze, finally, and seemed about to say something—maybe offer some reassurance, act like a normal mother for once. But she couldn't manage it, losing focus again almost immediately, and Jay felt silly for hoping for something more.

"There's hot dogs in the fridge," she said before closing her eyes again. After staring at her for a long moment, Jay snatched the spoiled orange juice off her nightstand and took it to the kitchen. This, at least, he could do for her. He poured it into the sink, watching it swirl down the drain, trying not to think of anything.

When the carton was empty, he stuffed it into their overflowing trash can. He knew he should take out the trash, but he was still freezing from his time in the water. Going outside again right then seemed like too much. Heading for the bedsheet curtain that marked a corner of the living room as his bedroom, he stripped off his wet shirt. As he shivered, he spotted a letter lying on his air mattress. "From Sergeant D. Moriarity" was printed on the envelope. He tightened his jaw at the sight of it, trying to stave off the chattering as he struggled out of his wet jeans. He didn't want to let the letter out of his sight, as though it might disappear like his father had. But he didn't want to open it, either.

After pulling on dry clothes, he trudged into the kitchen. He arranged a can of Vienna sausages, a bag of corn chips, and a bottle of ketchup on their scuffed kitchen table. Pulling each sausage directly from the can, he dipped it in ketchup, arranged it on a chip, and stuck the concoction in his mouth. Just another healthy homemade meal.

Throughout this routine, he kept his eyes fixed on his father's letter. Mid-bite, he grabbed a BIC lighter from among the clutter that covered the table and flicked it till a flame burst out. He slowly lowered it toward the envelope, but stopped before the fire touched the paper. He just couldn't do it. Even if he never read it—and he was pretty sure he never wanted to—he had to know that it was there. Maybe someday he would change his mind about it, or maybe not—but he wasn't ready to destroy the possibility just yet. Instead, he flipped the lighter closed and let it clatter onto the table.

Pushing his chair back, he carried the letter into his bedroom with him. Rummaging in the piles of clothes at the foot of his air mattress, he uncovered a cigar box and shoved the letter inside, where he wouldn't have to look at it every second. Then he shoved the box back under some clothes before flopping onto his bed. It wobbled beneath his weight, and he sighed. He always forgot that he couldn't treat his inflatable bed like a real bed, just like he couldn't treat this curtained-off corner like a real room. It just wasn't.

After yanking the curtain closed alongside his bed, he stretched out on top of his red comforter. Retrieving his notebook and pencil from just beneath the bed, he paused, wanting to sketch but not sure what to draw. He wasn't sure how to express his emotions about everything that had happened that day. An image popped into his mind, and he grinned and started re-creating it on the page. First he drew a giant, surging wave with the face of a lion. "Raaaaaawrrrrrr!" he muttered, pulled into the world of his drawing already. Next he drew Frosty surfing the wave, dressed like an ancient warrior—every bit as heroic as he'd looked when he pulled Jay from the sea. Propping the notebook against his bent knees, he let his imagination pour onto the page. The room grew dark as he sketched in the details, and he grabbed a flashlight, propped it up, and kept on drawing.

Sorting through his mail, Frosty stopped as he headed up his front walk. From inside, he heard his two-year-old daughter's shrieks as she struggled against bedtime. Watching his wife and daughter in silhouette through the curtains, he knew he should go in to help but couldn't bring himself to do it. He was sure Brenda could handle it, anyway. He told himself he would probably just be in the way.

With his headlights off and van idling, he backed out of the driveway, hoping that Roque's wails had masked the sound of him pulling in moments before. Parking down the street, he fixed his gaze on his house. The windows still glowed, signaling the activity within. To pass the time, he grabbed a copy of the *San Francisco Chronicle* from the seat beside him and turned to the crossword puzzle. With the paper spread across his lap, he peered at the clues under the light of a nearby streetlamp, glasses perched low on his nose. He turned the heater up, warming his hands over the vent. When he glanced up again, the window of Roque's room had finally gone dark. That was his cue. Pulling off his glasses, he flicked on the headlights and put the van in gear.

He coasted into the driveway and headed inside, shutting the front door softly behind him. In the kitchen, he opened the pantry, and the door dropped an inch from its hinge. Examining the stripped hinge, he made a mental note to fix it tomorrow, before retrieving a tin of coffee from the cupboard.

"Need a hand?" his wife asked, coming up behind him with a tired smile.

"With the cupboard or the coffee?" He smiled back, taking in her long, glossy dark hair, loose around her shoulders, her wide hazel eyes fixed on him, thinking how beautiful she was.

"You missed Roque again. I just got her down."

"Had to help a friend out after work. I'll go in and give her a kiss."

She gave him a curt nod, and he felt the strain between them. "Kiss would be nice. A conversation once in a while, even better." He tensed, thinking she would finally call him on his absentee parenting, order him to do better. But after a moment, she gave him the warm smile he had fallen in love with instead, diffusing the bite of her words.

With that, she turned to leave the room. Instead of relief at avoiding a confrontation, he felt smothered by regret. He knew he wasn't being the father he should be, but he didn't know how to do better. Seemed to him it was better to be an absent father than a bad one. Anyway, Brenda was the perfect mother—warm and down-to-earth, kind and attentive. She was what their daughter needed—not him.

CHAPTER 2

◀ ▶

The next morning, Jay emerged from behind the bedsheet to forage for breakfast.

His mom bustled in, wearing a white blouse and denim skirt, and swept the cashier's check from his dad off the counter. "How do I look?" she asked Jay shyly. "Tell the truth now. I got an interview with Sears."

"You look awesome," he told her, and meant it. He was glad his words made her smile. She looked better today—still tired but put together, her hair framing her face in soft blond waves, her eyes bright. His mom had gone through so many jobs since they moved here, it was hard to get too excited about a new one, but he liked seeing that she was.

"I'll be back at noon," she said. "Take you

shopping for school supplies. Wish me luck?"

"Good luck." Jay gave her an encouraging smile, hoping that this time, things really would work out.

He hung around the house all morning, clearing some of the junk off the kitchen table and counter, sorting through the clothing pile in his room, drawing in his notebook, throwing together some lunch. He wanted to be sure he was ready when his mom got home. It was only once the clock ticked a few minutes past noon that he started to worry. "Probably just running a little late," he muttered. He sat down at the kitchen table to wait, staring at the clock on the wall above it. He watched it till it read twelve thirty, then one fifteen. He got up, paced around the house, grabbed a handful of corn chips, dug a book out of his room, then slumped back at the table. He tried to read but he couldn't concentrate, looking from the clock to the door every few minutes as though he could will her to come home. Finally, at 2:35, he admitted to himself that she wasn't going to show.

He wandered outside, across the scraggly yard and into the garage. There, he flicked on the light to reveal piles of junk all the way up to the ceiling, covered in cobwebs. He scanned the piles, ignoring broken lamps and busted lawn chairs and tattered furniture, until finally he spotted the pale nose of a surfboard poking out near the rafters. He had figured that in a surfing town like Santa Cruz, every garage had at least one old surfboard stashed away in it. He was glad to see he had been right.

Jay grabbed a few crates and piled them up, climbing toward the ceiling. Although his tower teetered, he reached high above his head and balanced on his tiptoes to yank the surfboard free. When he realized it was only half a board, he was momentarily disappointed, but then he saw the other half gleaming nearby, with rags and old clothes stuffed all around it. He climbed back down, dragged the crate over, and retrieved the rest of the board from among the other junk.

Near the door, he retrieved a rusted red toolbox and rummaged through it until he found duct tape and epoxy. Sitting on the stained cement floor of the garage, he carefully glued the halves of the stained and dusty board together before binding them with the tape. It wasn't perfect, but he figured it would hold. At least, he hoped it would. But when he stood back to examine his work, he realized that the fin boxes at the bottom were missing. That wasn't something he could fix with tape and glue.

He trudged out of the garage, trailing his newly repaired board behind him. Leaving it leaning against the bungalow, he went inside to find something he could wear into the water. In his piles of clothes, he found a scuba top that his dad must have left behind. It was too big, but combined with his swimming trunks, it would have to do.

Back outside, he picked up the board and headed down the street to Frosty's. The board's tail scraped the pavement as he struggled to hold it high enough above the ground. When he reached the mailbox marked HESSON, he turned up the drive. He couldn't help but notice how nice their house looked with its fresh coat of white paint, compared with his own house with its paint stripped away by the salty sea breezes, gray wood showing through beneath.

On the lawn, two women in their late thirties were clipping the rosebushes. A two-year-old girl toddled around them, watering the lawn with a hose she dragged behind her.

"Excuse me, ma'am?" Standing at the curb,

Jay looked from one woman to the other, unsure of which one to address. "Your husband home?" He hobbled toward them, his board banging against the ground.

"Depends on who's asking," said the one with the long dark hair, standing up to meet him.

"I'm Jay Moriarity, ma'am." He held out his hand. "He saved my life yesterday."

She grasped his hand briefly, but confusion clouded her hazel eyes. "I think you might be mistaken. Frosty was laying a roof up in Scotts Valley yesterday."

"No, ma'am, he was out surfing at Three Mile. At the exact same time I used up my 'lotment of dumb luck."

"Is that right?" Frosty's wife sighed, and it occurred to Jay that maybe Frosty hadn't wanted her to know about his surfing excursion. Now he felt bad—leave it to him to get his hero into trouble. No wonder Frosty hadn't wanted anything more to do with him.

Grinning, her curly-haired friend leaned over and stage-whispered to the little girl, "Your father? Surfing? Noooo . . ."

The girl giggled, though she surely didn't get the joke, and her mom couldn't help smiling, too.

"Well, Frosty happens to be out at the Point right now. So is there something I can do for you, Jay Moriarity?"

He nodded, his expression earnest. "I was hoping to learn the sport of kings today, but I seem to be missing parts from the bottom of my board." He held up the broken board for her to see.

"Sport of kings, huh? You *have* been talking to my husband." She gave her friend a knowing smile. "Zeuf, could you watch Roque for a minute?" When her neighbor nodded, Frosty's wife gave Jay a friendly smile. "I'm Brenda, by the way. Follow me, sweetie. Let's see what we can do."

Jay followed Brenda down the driveway and over the footpath behind the house. He admired the lush green grass, so different from his own yard with its scattered patches of yellow grass, weeds, and dirt. As he walked, he kept trying to tuck in the flapping neoprene tail of his oversize shirt, but it kept pulling free again.

When they reached a shed in the back, Brenda flung open the door. Jay stood transfixed in the doorway, taking in the surfboards in every size and color racked on the walls and across the rafters. While Brenda rummaged in the drawers of a large red tool cabinet, Jay zeroed in on a bright red ten-foot board, its nose sharp as a spear. It was spectacular, truly a board for doing battle with the waves.

While he stared at the board, Brenda stood up, triumphant, slamming a metal drawer shut with a clang. She handed him three small fins, exactly what he needed to finish repairing his board. Noticing the direction of his gaze, she smiled again. "They call that a gun, don't ask me why. It's for riding the really big ones. Monsters, like that." She gestured to a photo of Frosty shooting down a thirty-foot wall of ominous black water. Jay stared at the picture in amazement. He knew instantly he wanted to do that, exactly that—that he wouldn't stop until he at least got the chance to try.

After Brenda helped him wedge the fins onto the board, he headed down East Cliff Drive toward Pleasure Point. As he made his way down the old wooden staircase to the beach, he kept his eyes fixed on the watery horizon.

At one of the landings, he saw a group of dangerous-looking boys hanging out beneath the stairwell. While one carved his initials into the steps with a pocketknife, another, a local thug named Sonny Purrier, turned to scowl at Jay. Sonny was only twelve, but he towered over eight-year-old Jay—and even if he hadn't, his constantly seething fury would have made him plenty intimidating. "Beat it, Little Trash!" he shouted.

Jay didn't know why the older boy called him that, didn't even know if the kid actually knew who he was, or just said that to every boy he saw. But he knew it was best to avoid Sonny if he could, that confronting him would mean nothing but trouble.

Averting his gaze, Jay continued down the stairs. He passed homeless men sitting on the tiered seawall, their eyes glassed over. Some of them begged for change, while others huddled alongside the crumbling cement wall, ragged coats pulled over them as they slept. He slowed to take in the words SURF WHERE YOU LIVE spray painted on the wall in giant green bubble letters. Everyone knew how territorial surfers were in Santa Cruz, but he didn't understand why. There was plenty of ocean for everyone, and it wasn't like anyone could actually possess that giant expanse of water. He had never seen the point to fighting over it.

Making his way across the slippery rocks at the edge of the ocean, Jay passed a trio of surfers around his own age. They whispered and pointed at him as he passed. Glancing down at his thrown-together, mismatched outfit with his shirt bunched and flapping, he knew he didn't fit in with these young surfers in their fullsuits and surf booties. But he didn't care. So what if they could afford nice gear when he could afford, well, nothing? It shouldn't matter. He just wanted to surf, same as them.

Turning his gaze to the ocean, he watched a flock of young surfers paddling out toward waves that glinted in the sun. Out toward the horizon, he caught sight of Frosty's distinctive mane of wavy dark-blond hair as he knee paddled down the coast on his longboard. As Jay watched, the man stroked inland as an outside wave began to form and dropped into its glassy peak. With athletic precision, he did a quick cross-step before fluidly accelerating across the pitching wave. As Frosty cut through the crowd of young surfers, Jay beamed at the surf god's relaxed style, his fingers skimming the shimmering water as though calibrating the wave. Jay felt himself filled to the depths of his soul with yearning to do what Frosty did.

Entering the icy water, Jay tried to paddle through the shore break but was tossed right off his board. He remounted, but his weight was too far back, tilting the board toward the sky like a seesaw. Frosty made surfing look easy, but now that he was out on the water by himself, it was immediately apparent to Jay that it was not.

By the time he reached the line of young surfers, Jay's lips were purple with cold, and he shivered in his oversize shirt. The surfers glared at him, and although he felt their contempt radiating toward him, his smile never faltered. All he wanted was to be out here, to try.

But although he didn't care what they thought of him, he couldn't have cared more about Frosty's opinion. Glancing back at the shore, Jay saw the man watching him as he shook the water from his thick hair. Now Jay knew he had to do something to impress the older surfer.

"Outside!" one of the young surfers shouted. A set of waves loomed above them, and everyone started paddling. The first wave of the set crashed over Jay, smashing his board into his mouth and tossing him into the air.

As he struggled to recover, a boy about his age paddled over, taking pity on him. "Hey, man, you gotta go in. You're bleeding."

Jay looked at the freckled boy with sun-bleached hair and tried to smile. But when he did, he felt the blood trickling from his lip. "Can't. Not until I get up."

"Dude." The kid shook his head. "It's not like that. Believe me, nobody gets up their first time."

Despite the blood gushing from his lip, Jay mustered an expression of pure determination. "I will."

The other boy glanced toward a small set that was rolling in and seemed to make a decision. He grabbed Jay's board and turned it to face the beach. "Okay. But I'm only doing this because you're gonna start attracting sharks with all that blood. I say 'now,' you paddle as hard as you can."

Sliding nimbly off his own board, the blond kid grabbed the tail of Jay's. "Soon as you feel the wave take you, pretend like you're doing a push-up, then get to your feet. Got it?"

Jay nodded and readied himself as best he could. Everything seemed to happen in slow motion now as he waited for his moment.

"Now?" he asked.

"No," the blond boy told him.

"Now?" It had to be now. The waves were so close.

"No."

"Now?" He didn't know how he could wait another second.

"Now!" the kid shouted. "Paddle, paddle, paddle!"

Jay paddled as hard as he could as the blond boy gave him a shove into the wave. It propelled Jay upward, and he pushed to his feet. As he crested and began the two-foot drop, he thought that this had to be the best feeling in the world. He never wanted it to end.

CHAPTER 3

◀ ▶

1994

So he didn't let it. He built up to bigger and bigger waves, and by the time he was fifteen, he was taking on twelve-foot drops, no problem. He was out on the waves again today, launching himself from the peak on his longboard—still a used one, but better than the one he had cobbled together as a kid. His blue eyes flashed with the pure thrill of the drop, the wind whooshing through his close-cropped curls. Setting a rail, he ripped a deep bottom turn, completely in control of the wave. He drove off the lip, and a canopy of spray showered him as he carved down the line, moving up and down the face of the wave while staying ahead of the break. As he reached the critical section, the most challenging part of the ride, he cross-stepped the nose, walking along the length of his longboard while remaining steady on his feet. He arched his back, curling the toes of his front foot around the nose of his blue-and-white board, his other foot braced behind him as he hung five.

In one fluid motion, he kicked off the back of the wave and onto his board, paddling past a young boy scrapping for the next wave of the set. Reaching over, Jay helped launch him onto the wave with a gentle shove to the tail of the boy's board. Jay's smile broadened as he watched the kid catch the wave and get to his feet. It always made him happy to help out another surfer. Continuing to the shore, Jay spotted his friend, Blond Brown, in the shallows, his orange shortboard tucked under his arm.

"Stealing a page outta my playbook, huh?" Blond called to him, grinning.

"Can't help myself, Blondie. It's always been a good one." Without an assist from Blond on his first day out, who knew how long it would have taken Jay to ride his first wave. He would always be grateful to his friend for helping him learn to surf. When he reached Blond's side, the two of them left the surf and headed for the steps.

As they neared the top, they saw Sonny Purrier, now eighteen, his hair slicked back and scraggly facial hair shadowing his face. Perched on the bluff's railing with his crew, he clutched a baseball bat, idly banging it against the rail. Jay noticed that Sonny had a new tattoo, a black shield emblazoned on the side of his neck with an ES in its center, designating him as an Eastside surfer. There was so much rivalry between the different surfing contingents in town, and Jay still didn't see the point of it. It seemed to him that they should all be on the same team.

But guys like Sonny didn't think that way. "All play and no work makes Blond a very broke boy." Sonny pointed the bat at Blond accusingly before turning to Jay. "Ain't that right, Little Trash?"

Jay had no idea what the guy was talking about. "Whatever you say, man," he replied with a shrug. Sonny was always worked up about something. No point trying to figure out what it was this time.

They reached the top of the steps, and Sonny stuck out his bat to block Jay from passing. "So . . . I got a question. What exactly are you trying to prove with that longboard of yours?" He gestured lewdly out from his black board shorts as his crew of hoods cracked up.

"Was about to ask you the same thing about your bat." Jay gave him a long look before pushing past him. Out of the corner of his eye, he saw Sonny start to come after him, but he stopped as a Santa Cruz Police Department squad car slowly cruised past.

Sonny backed off, shouting after Jay and Blond instead of chasing them. "Y'all come back now, ya hear?"

As they continued down the coast road, Jay asked, "What was that supposed to mean about no work making you a broke boy?"

He thought he saw a flash of anxiety on his friend's face, but Blond just said, "It's Sonny Purrier, man. Who knows what goes on inside that guy's head." Jay thought that was as good an explanation as any, though he had a sneaking suspicion that Blond had understood Sonny's words better than he would admit.

When they crossed onto 38th Street, Blond abruptly stopped and elbowed Jay. Turning, Jay saw Kim, now seventeen and gorgeous, climbing into a VW bus painted with psychedelic images of busty mermaids and flowing waves.

"Hey, Kim," Jay called.

She turned to look at him, blond hair fanning out as she spun, and her smile lit up her face. "Hey, you. How was it out there?"

"Um, good, really good." He felt nervous talking to her now, like he never had when they were kids. It seemed to matter so much now that she was older, that he was a lowly sophomore while she was a cool senior. But he jumped on this rare chance to talk to her and did his best to draw it out. "Feels like the swell's building."

"How do ya know? You *time* it?" They both laughed, and suddenly he didn't feel awkward with her anymore. It felt just like it had when they were little, just two best friends who did everything together.

Then a guy called from the van, "Kimmy, come on, we gotta go."

Jay glanced inside to see the van tightly packed with older teenage girls and guys. He recognized a few of them—cool older surfers and their girlfriends, a group who never spoke to him even though they surfed the same spots. It hit him then that fifteen really was very young, and the realization stung. He couldn't drive yet, and even if he could, he wouldn't have been able to afford a car or been able to pay to take her on a date. Assuming, of course, she would even have been willing to go. How could he expect to compete with the older guys who flocked around her, all just as aware of her beauty as he was? He knew he couldn't.

"Maybe I'll see you out there, okay?" Kim gave him a quick wave before hopping into the red van, already giggling with her friends. Jay held up his hand in reply, though he knew she wouldn't see.

Blond shook his head. "'Let it be,' dude. . . . 'Speaking words of wisdom.'"

Jay nodded at the insightfulness of the Beatles' lyrics, but he couldn't help himself. He would always feel drawn to Kim, he knew it, even if he was just a kid to her now.

They were almost to his house when a scream pierced the air. Jay broke into a run, barely registering the neighbors emerging from their houses as the screams continued. To his horror, he realized they were coming from his house. He burst through the screen door to find his mom huddled on the kitchen floor. Their current tenant, Eli, stood over her. The forty-something biker whirled to face Jay, his long, greasy hair whipping around as he turned.

"Easy, boy. This is about back rent, is all." He wobbled, clearly drunk, as he moved toward Jay. "She tried to grab at me, and all I did was defend myself—"

Jay didn't need to hear another word. He launched himself at Eli, sending them both hurtling over the countertop, knocking beer cans and a small surfing trophy to the floor. The plastic trophy broke in pieces, and even though it was one of his most treasured possessions, Jay was too furious to care.

Jay threw the older man through the open front door. Grasping Eli's shirt collar with one hand to keep him close, Jay wound up to punch the man with the other. But Blond grabbed his arm, struggling to hold him back, though Jay struggled just as hard against him, landing a few blows on Eli as he did. All the neighbors watched silently from their lawns, and Jay felt embarrassment build on top of his fury. Still, it wasn't enough to make him stop. Eli had hurt his mom, and he had to pay for that. After all, Jay was the only one she had left to protect her.

An SCPD squad car screeched to a stop, and

two officers jumped out. Just then, Jay spotted Frosty standing in the middle of the street, watching it all. Their eyes locked for a moment, but Jay was too ashamed to hold the gaze. He dropped his eyes, and his fists, all the will to fight going out of him. He had seen Frosty's disapproval, and he couldn't bear that. Sure, he had just been protecting his mom, but he knew he had gone too far, carried away by his rage.

While he talked to the police, while he comforted his mom and made sure she was okay, while he cleaned up the mess that the fight had made of their apartment, all Jay could think of was how bad he wanted to get back out on the ocean. That was the only place where things made sense.

Once he had settled his mom into bed, he slipped out of the house, trudging with his board down to the Pleasure Point Ravine. Clutching his longboard, he raced down a riverbed cut between the cliffs, leaping from rock to rock. When he reached the beach, he hurled himself into the shore break. Stroking outside the break, he sat up on his board. He splashed water over his face to keep himself alert as he stared out at the stars.

He didn't know how long he stayed out there,

trying not to even think, trying to just be at one with the ocean beneath him and the stars above, but finally he forced himself to head back in. His mom might need something, and anyway, he had to be up for school in the morning.

He walked slowly toward home, not wanting to return but knowing he had to eventually. He noticed that the door to their rental unit stood open, the interior eerily empty when it had been brimming with Eli's stuff only hours before. At least that guy was gone for good. He just hoped their next tenant wouldn't be even worse.

Inside, Jay curled up on his air mattress behind the relative privacy of the bedsheet curtain, not even bothering to change out of his red hooded sweatshirt and jeans. He noticed that his mom had propped his surfing trophy beside his bed. It had been so broken in the scuffle that he hadn't been sure it was worth repairing. But she had put it back together with Q-tips and superglue, and while it wasn't perfect, he had to smile at her effort. 1ST PLACE, LONGBOARD DIVISION— JAY MORIARITY, it read. It was his first surfing trophy, and he felt a wash of relief that, however damaged, it had been saved.

CHAPTER 4

◀ ▶

Though he fell into a fast and deep sleep, he was startled awake by the whine of an engine outside. He glanced at his alarm clock: 4:01 a.m. Peering out the front window, he saw Frosty down the street, loading the red gun into his van. If Frosty was taking out the board he used to surf monster waves, that meant there must be some monster waves to catch.

Jay ran outside, chasing Frosty's van through the fog. He had to see this. Grabbing hold of the ladder attached to the van's rear door, he hoisted himself up. Through the window, he saw Frosty sipping his coffee, oblivious to his new passenger. Jay knew Frosty would send him home if he saw him, so he climbed onto the roof, determined to stay out of sight.

He heard the radio blaring out a surfing conditions report. "Be advised there is a high surf advisory in effect. Buoys reporting twenty feet at sixteen seconds with swells west-by-northwest at two hundred, ninety-five degrees . . ."

The van swerved past a Highway 1 North sign, and Jay's eyes widened. He hadn't expected to have to hang on to the roof on the freeway. With a whoosh, they swung onto the highway, and Jay grinned, thrilled at the wind in his hair as they sped along. Headlights from the opposite direction flashed across his face and he laughed, wondering if any of the other drivers had noticed him clinging to the roof and what they thought if they had.

Frosty turned off the highway and wound through a dilapidated harbor. In the early-morning mist, Jay made out the forms of rotting piers with weathered old fishing boats tethered to them. A foghorn blew mournfully in the distance, from some unseen boat. He saw Frosty wave to a grizzled old fisherman. With a nod, the man unfastened a chain that blocked access further into the harbor, allowing the van to pass.

"Morning, Frank," Frosty called to the man.

"Careful out there, son," Frank replied as Frosty drove by.

Soon they were bumping along a dirt road, and Jay finally slid off the back of the van. Crouching in the tall weeds beside the path, Jay noticed a sign reading PILLAR POINT. He had expected to tag along with Frosty to some popular surfing spot, not somewhere he had never heard of. But now he was really determined to see what the older surfer was up to.

He watched Frosty park next to two trucks. Three huge, rugged men climbed out of the pickups to meet him. As they suited up and waxed their spearlike boards, they looked like warriors to Jay—their frames powerful, their eyes cool and calculating. He crept through the weeds to get close enough to hear them.

"Twenty-five at sixteen, ladies," said one of the surfers. "Rock 'n' roll."

The four men headed down a pathway that wound along the edge of a towering cliff. Jay followed, keeping a safe distance behind to avoid being detected. Below, the waves pounded against the rocks, loud as thunder. When the men reached the inky water's edge, they paddled out into the ominously choppy water. Atop their surfboards, they glided past rock formations that pierced the ocean's dark surface like steeples of an alien underworld.

Jay had to find a way to watch the men surf the massive waves he saw cresting in the distance, but he knew he couldn't let them see him. There was nowhere to hide down by the shore, so he turned to the cliff above him. It would be a precipitous climb of two hundred feet or more, but if he wanted to see what he had come here for, it was his only option. With a deep breath, he grabbed on to the nearest handholds and started to climb. On his way up, he slid on a patch of loose dirt, sending a spray of pebbles clattering downward, but caught himself before he followed them to the ground far below. After steadying himself and finding solid ledges to grab on to, he continued his climb.

At the top, he found himself facing three enormous white satellite dishes, each five stories tall, tilted toward the sky. They were surrounded by a barbed-wire fence, which looked starkly primitive beside their high-tech grandeur. He wondered where on earth he had ended up.

But there was something even more magnificent to see in the ocean below. As the sun began to tinge the sky orange with the fiery tendrils of sunrise, he turned to see massive waves like rolling mountains churning below. He gasped, mouth falling open in sheer amazement. The monster waves, smooth and black as polished ebony, rose up as far as he could see out across the ocean. Each of them had to be twenty or thirty feet high—the biggest waves he'd ever seen. To reach this size, they must have traveled a thousand miles across the sea, gaining force along their journey before detonating in a mass of foaming water against this shore. The waves slammed against the cliff with a resounding *boom!* that sent vibrations up through his feet and, it seemed to him, straight to his heart. These were the waves he'd dreamed of, and he knew that he had to find a way to ride them himself.

"Swing wide! Paddle, paddle, paddle!" one of the surfers screamed above the roar of the waves.

As Jay watched, the four men paddled up, up, endlessly up the straight vertical face of a twenty-five-foot bomb, defying gravity itself. They cleared the lip of the wave with no time to spare, and plummeted directly into the trough of nature's own wild roller coaster. Frosty and the others cleared the second wave and moved into position. At the peak, Frosty took off, his eyes narrowed in concentration, every inch the master of the wave. He made the drop, his rumbling "Yee-haw!" audible across the water. He looked tiny against the gigantic black mountain he rode, arcing across the base of the mammoth as he shot down the line, an explosion of whitewater churning at his heels. It looked like he was outrunning an avalanche.

Jay soaked up every death-defying, awe-inspiring move, the roar of the monster waves echoing in his ears. He had known Frosty was a great surfer, but now he saw the man was a titan, a lord of the sea, a legend. As Frosty kicked off the wave, he glanced over his shoulder and looked straight at Jay atop the bluffs. With his fists in the air, reveling in the glorious surfing he had just witnessed, Jay felt the older man's eyes lock with his. He had been spotted, and even from this distance, he could feel the sting of Frosty's glare. Lowering his arms, he began his climb back down to the shore. Though he was nervous about facing Frosty's wrath, he was still buzzing with excitement. Those waves, these surfers, were the most amazing thing he had ever seen, and he wouldn't have traded that experience for anything.

Once he reached the shore, Frosty waved

good-bye to the other surfers, focused now on dealing with Jay. Marching Jay back to his van, he motioned Jay into the passenger seat and loaded his own board without a word. Jay didn't dare to say anything, either. It wasn't until they were back on Highway 1 that Frosty broke the silence.

"We'll agree to forget how you got up here." Frosty wrung his hands on the wheel, a ball of barely contained energy. "But as far as most are concerned, that wave—Mavericks—that's a myth, like the Loch Ness Monster. And we intend to keep it that way. Is that clear?"

Still not sure he was allowed to speak, Jay simply nodded.

The shortwave radio crackled to life. "Be advised buoys reporting twenty-two feet at eighteen seconds with swells—" it began, but Frosty snapped off the radio.

"Just how big was that wave?" Jay asked, unable to keep quiet anymore. He had to know.

"Did you hear what I said?" Frosty demanded.

"Yes, sir. Loch Ness Monster." Jay waited a long moment for Frosty to say something more, before finally asking again, "But how big *was* that monster?"

Frosty shook his head, knobby knuckles white as he gripped the steering wheel. Watching him closely, Jay saw that the man was clenching his jaw as though trying to hold back a response. But he never said another word, the whole drive back to his place, and Jay thought it best not to push the man any further. He knew he was lucky that Frosty wasn't screaming at him, or threatening to tell Christy what he had done. In the grand scheme of things, the silent treatment wasn't so bad.

When they reached Frosty's driveway, he pulled the van in and began unloading his gear. Jay got out to help, but Frosty waved him off. Feeling useless, Jay watched Frosty move from van to shed with the easy efficiency of long practice. Finally, the surfer seemed to notice Jay again and motioned toward the boy's bungalow. "You, uh . . . you all right down there?"

Jay ducked his head. Besides witnessing his fight with Eli, he was sure Frosty had seen the myriad of bottomfeeders who had made their homes in the bungalow's back unit over the years. "Mom's not renting out the back anymore. Means I get my own room, but gotta double up my shifts at Pleasure Pizza." It had been such a relief when

Christy announced that they would manage somehow without a tenant. One less thing for Jay to worry about, and for the first time since his dad left, a real room to call his own.

"And your father?" Frosty sounded reluctant, like he knew the answer would give him more information than he really wanted.

"He sent me a letter a couple years back." Jay shrugged as they headed toward the surf shed, trying to say as little as possible. "From his base in Panama."

"So what'd he say? In the letter."

"Don't know. Never opened it." Jay heard the defiance in his own voice and didn't care. He wanted Frosty to know, wanted everyone to know, that whatever his dad had to say to him didn't matter one bit.

Frosty looked away, suddenly uncomfortable. "Look, I gotta get to work—"

But Jay wasn't going to let him get away again. "I wanna take that drop, Frosty. Ride that wave." For the past seven years, he'd been trying to find a way to ask Frosty to teach him to surf monsters, but he had never mustered the courage to try. Maybe this wasn't the perfect time, but he had to take his chance. He might not get another one.

Frosty leaned his board against the wall of his surf shed, turning to face Jay. "Not gonna happen."

"Why not?" Jay demanded.

"'Cuz untrained boys don't step in the ring with Mike Tyson, that's why." He flung open the door of the shed, but then turned to see the heartbroken expression on Jay's face.

"We've been surfing that break for years. And the bigger the wave, the greater the amount of water needed to produce it. And the more strength and know-how needed to survive it. You don't have the *strength*, and you don't have the *know-how*. Period." He kept explaining, but Jay just kept staring at him, blue eyes full of pleading. Frosty sighed. "Here, take my hand." He held up one massive hand, and Jay hesitated. "Go on."

Jay took it, his small hand devoured by Frosty's meaty paw.

"Now resist. Put your body into it." Frosty pushed him against the side of the shed, bending Jay's hand at the wrist. Jay resisted with all his might, but he was no match for Frosty. "Come on, is that all you got?"

Using both hands now, Jay groaned with the effort of fending Frosty off, the veins bulging in his lean arms. But there was nothing he could do. Frosty effortlessly pinned him against the wall.

"Okay . . . Okay!" Jay shouted, and Frosty let go.

Jay grabbed his forearm, wincing from the strain. "Look, right now I'm surfing every—"

Frosty didn't let him finish. "Shut up, all right. I'm serious." Jay started to respond, but Frosty held up a hand to stop him. "I know how good you are, I've seen you out there. You surf circles around those other kids, but those are *normal* waves. Surfing normal waves is about how you perform when everything goes *right*. Big-wave riding is about how you perform when everything goes *wrong*. And on days like today, you don't wanna *know* wrong."

The words sent a shiver down Jay's spine. He could feel the truth of them.

"One bump off that lip'll pitch you headfirst over the falls, and at that height, it's like hitting concrete at fifty. A thousand tons of ocean coming down on top of you, ripping you apart, knocking you senseless, and driving you into a place so deep and so dark . . ." His expression turned inward, as though he were reliving the experience he described. "You don't wanna know."

Jay held the older man's gaze for a moment, then asked simply, "So why do it?"

Frosty turned away, breaking the connection Jay was sure they had just shared. He stepped into the backyard, turning a hose on his wetsuit. "Get outta here, will you? I got a roof to lay."

Ignoring the attempted brush-off, Jay insisted, "Train me, then. To ride it, I mean."

Frosty met Jay's unblinking stare with a burst of laughter. "Wrong guy. Like I said, beat it."

Knowing he had pushed as far as he could, Jay trotted obediently down the driveway. So maybe Frosty would never be his teacher, he thought. There had to be some other way to learn to ride those waves.

CHAPTER 5

◀ ▶

Once the kid was out of sight, Frosty turned off the hose and headed for the house. Brenda stood in the open kitchen doorway, their eight-month-old baby, Lake, cradled in her arms.

"You don't get it, do you?" She shook her head at him disapprovingly before ducking back into the house. He hadn't even noticed her there before, but he realized now that she must have overheard his entire conversation with Jay.

Frosty followed her inside, down the hall, and into Lake's room. He stood in the doorway, watching her lay their son down in his crib and smooth a blanket over him.

"Get what? What're you talking about?" he demanded.

"Shhhhhh," she whispered, pointing to the baby. After leaning in to give Lake a kiss, she eased out of the room and softly shut the door behind her.

"There are all kinds of sons, Frosty," she told him, leading the way into the living room. "Some are born to you, others just . . . occur to you. That boy's looked up to you his whole life. Can't you see how much he needs you?"

"Whoa, whoa, wait a minute," he protested. "You don't even want me surfing that wave."

"You're right. And you continue to break that promise every chance you get." She looked up, piercing him with her gaze. "I know where you surfed this morning. Heard the message on the machine. 'Twenty-five at sixteen . . .'"

"Okay, I don't know where this is going, but I'm late for work." He walked away, but Brenda kept talking as though he hadn't moved.

"That boy's gonna do it anyway. You know that, don't you? Even if he dies trying."

Frosty turned back to face her, and she drove her point home. "I mean, wouldn't you?"

He knew she was right. She almost always was. But that didn't mean he had to like it.

Thanks to his wife's words, he spent all day

trying to shake the image of the kid's pleading blue eyes. But he already had a son he didn't know what to do with, and a daughter, too—and now she wanted him to take in some stray? The boy needed a father figure, that was obvious to anyone even halfway paying attention, but that for sure wasn't him. Of course the kid had looked up to him ever since he saved his life, that was only natural, but you would think Jay would have gotten the hint after all these years. Seven years since they met, living less than a block apart, moving in the same surfing circles, and they had only spoken a handful of times. Did the kid really think that was coincidence? But now it seemed like his days of dodging the boy were over. Now that Brenda had taken an interest, she would make sure of that if Frosty didn't do it himself.

Once his roofing work was done for the day, Frosty camped out in his surf shed, sitting in his old brown recliner and blasting Jefferson Airplane while he spread epoxy on a damaged rail of the board he had used that morning.

He looked up when Brenda entered, brandishing Jay's red hoodie sweatshirt. "Someone left this in your van."

Frosty looked away without a word. Shaking

her head at him again, she tossed the shirt on the bench and left.

Perspiration beaded his brow as he tended to his board. When he paused, his gaze fixed on the framed photo of him dropping down the same vertical ledge of black water he had surfed that morning: Mavericks. Nothing else like it in the world.

He screwed the lids back on the now-empty cans of resin and hardener and strode out of the shed. Out back, he stuck them both on a shelf. A graveyard of destroyed guns were piled along his shed's back wall, some boards snapped in two, others gutted down the stringer, all hit with such excessive force that looking at them made you wonder how the rider had survived. Of course, Frosty knew the answer: barely, by the skin of his teeth.

It was clear to him now that, just as Brenda had said, he had no choice but to help the kid. Of course Jay would try big-wave surfing, with or without him—and without him, the kid wouldn't have a chance. That shouldn't be his problem, but since he was the one who had exposed the kid to monsters—however unwillingly—it seemed it was his responsibility anyway. Storming back into the shed, Frosty snatched the boy's hoodie off the bench where Brenda had left it and headed for his van. He drove fast to Pleasure Pizza, where the kid had said he worked. No point in delaying the inevitable.

In the hot kitchen of Pleasure Pizza, Jay ladled sauce onto a massive pie. His friend Blond manned the register, shouting orders back to him. "One sausage and olive, one regular," he called. The phone started ringing, and Jay saw people crowded into the cavelike hangout and a line that went out the door. The customers ogled the photos of surfing greats that plastered the walls as they chatted beneath the ship-wheel chandeliers that dangled from the ceiling. It was packed out there, but it was suffocating here behind the counter, as Blond dashed back and forth with orders and Jay struggled to keep up.

Blond grabbed the ladle out of his hand, jarring Jay out of his thoughts as a spray of sauce spattered his apron. "First sauce, then cheese, then toppings. It's not rocket science."

Jay looked down at the pizza he had been

making, a layer of sauce puddled on top of the shredded cheese, and sighed.

"You all right?" Blond asked, concern flashing across his face. "You haven't been here since you got here, man."

"Yeah . . . no, I'm fine. Just thinking." Jay's mind was too full of the things he wanted but could not have to leave room for mundane tasks like pizza making. But he figured he owed his friend an explanation—after all, Blond had gotten him this job. And who knew, maybe his buddy would understand. "You ever see something and feel like it's why you were put here? I mean, on this earth?"

Blond nodded, looking introspective for once. "Sure, man. Every time I turn on *Baywatch*." He clapped Jay on the back, grinning. He turned to see a cluster of twelve-year-old girls hovering at the counter, fawning over Jay.

"Hey, keep it moving! Next!" he told them, shooing them away. Jay thought he caught a look of jealousy on Blond's face. No one wanted a gaggle of preteen groupies, but then again, he had to admit the attention was flattering. And the girls always seemed to be staring at him—never his buddy. Of course that wouldn't be fun to see, night after night.

Outside, a car horn blared, and Jay looked up to see Frosty's white van double-parked out front. He couldn't believe it, and knew he didn't have a moment to lose.

He ducked under the counter and dashed for the door, while Blond called after him. "Dude! What're you doing now? You're killing me here!"

But Jay didn't pause to answer, just kept pushing his way through the crowd.

Once he got outside and neared the van, Frosty rolled down the passenger window. "Hey . . ." Jay faltered, unsure of what to say. Of course he hoped Frosty was here to suddenly offer to teach him how to surf the big waves, but he didn't really dare to let himself hope for that.

The older man scrutinized him, his gaze unrelenting, seeming to take in every flaw. But finally, he spoke. "Okay, here's the deal. I'll train you for one thing, and one thing only. To survive that wave. You wanna know why?"

Stunned into silence, Jay just stared.

"'Cuz I don't want it on my conscience. But that's it—no questions, no arguing, end of story.

I teach you what you need to know and it's over. After that you go off and break your neck, get a terminal shark bite, I don't wanna know about it. Got it?"

All Jay could do was nod. "Got it."

"Reason no one knows about Mavericks is it only breaks on big northwest swells. And we'll be lucky if there's twelve weeks of that left this year." Fixing Jay with his intense gaze, Frosty told him, "So you got twelve weeks."

Frosty tossed the red hoodie at him, and Jay snatched it out of the air. "Meet me at my shed, six thirty tomorrow morning. Not six thirty-one or six thirty-two." With that, Frosty gunned his van, swerving back into the flow of traffic.

Jay watched him go, his shock slowly melting away as an enormous grin spread across his face. It was mind-blowing to think that in twelve weeks he might be getting up on one of those monster waves. He might have stayed in that spot for the rest of the evening if Blond hadn't leaned out the door, shouting that he needed help inside. Jay dashed back into the frenzy of demanding customers, but all night long, his smile never faded.

CHAPTER 6

◀ ▶

Early the next morning, Jay rolled up to Frosty's shed on his skateboard. Standing in the doorway, he saw the older man pulling on a rash guard, eyes locked on a digital clock that read "six thirty." Jay saw Frosty grimace, and knew he'd better make his presence known before the clock ticked off one minute more.

"Morning." He kicked off his skateboard, balancing his surfboard under his arm while he rifled through his backpack for his full wetsuit.

"Don't bother. We're not surfing." Frosty turned off the heater that hummed in the corner of the shed and joined Jay outside. He gestured to two fourteen-foot paddleboards, one red and one orange, lying in the grass beside the shed. They were the kind beach lifeguards used, each with a compass and water-bottle cage affixed to the front. After sliding a water bottle into each cage, Frosty motioned for Jay to pick up a board.

Jay knew better by now than to question Frosty, so he simply stuffed the wetsuit back into his backpack and tossed the bag into the shed. Leaving his surfboard leaning against the wall, he picked up a paddleboard.

Both barefoot and in board shorts, he and Frosty lugged the boards down 38th Street, through the foggy darkness. Although Frosty toted the huge board with ease, Jay teetered under its awkward bulk. Still, he was determined to keep up, without complaint.

"A few things we need to establish before we begin," Frosty said.

Startled at the man's voice in the silent early morning, Jay whipped around to look at him, pivoting the board with him. Its tail slapped into the antenna of a parked car, and Jay jerked it back, hoping he hadn't done any real damage. It wasn't like he could afford to pay for car repairs.

Taking in the scene, Frosty told him, "First: Thou shalt not ding Frosty's boards or damage thy neighbor's car."

"Yes, sir, sorry." Jay examined both the car

and the board, and was relieved to see that they both looked okay.

"Second: This little, uh, *program* is about building what I call the four pillars of a solid human foundation. Understand?" Frosty stopped his march toward the ocean to look at Jay, waiting for his response.

Jay nodded obediently, which only earned him a scowl.

"How could you? I haven't even told you what they are." Frosty kept walking, leaving Jay to stumble along behind him. Reaching the wooden staircase that led down to the beach, Frosty lifted the board effortlessly above his head and started down, while Jay struggled to do the same.

"Lemme ask you—how many legitimate big-wave riders do you think there are in the world? Guys who can paddle into twenty-five-foot-plus waves." Jay opened his mouth to answer, but Frosty didn't give him a chance to take a guess. "Less than a hundred, and most are the same: guys who've been given God's gift, but can't articulate an intelligent thought."

They reached the beach, wading together into the misty shallows, the chill instantly seeping into their skin.

"Is that the kind of individual you wanna be?" Frosty demanded. "Someone who can ride a great mountain of water, but whose soul is as shallow as a puddle?"

"No, sir," Jay replied without a moment's hesitation.

Frosty gave a quick nod, slid onto his knees, and began paddling with both arms. Jay did the same, trying to match the other man's long, rhythmic strokes.

"Okay, then, here we go. Deep breaths, steady rhythm, drive and glide."

Jay paddled after him, out into the fog. As the sun began to rise, the mist glowed golden, a magical haze.

"Steady as she goes . . . and breathe. You need to stretch out those lungs. A wave like Mavericks'll hold you down for minutes at a time, while it pounds you to a pulp." Frosty glanced back at Jay to make sure he was keeping up and catching his words. "If you can't hold your breath for at least four minutes under normal circumstances, you may as well not even paddle out."

Jay nodded, determined to show Frosty that he wasn't just some dumb kid. He rolled off his board with a splash, disappearing underwater.

But just a moment later, he burst back to the surface, gulping in air with big, heaving breaths. "How long was that?" he gasped.

Frosty sat up on his board, shaking his head in disapproval. "You know, I'm not even gonna acknowledge that just happened." He simply lay back down on his board and began paddling again.

Before long, Jay was struggling along, forty yards behind Frosty, panting with the strain. "How much farther?"

"How far do you think we've paddled?" Frosty called over his shoulder.

"I don't know—a thousand miles?" Jay's arms ached and his chest burned. After years of spending every spare moment surfing, he had been sure he could handle anything Frosty threw at him. Now it was clear that he wasn't even close to ready for the monsters he wanted to ride. But that just meant he would have to work harder. That, he could do.

Slowing to a glide on the glassy surface of the sea, Frosty grabbed his water bottle and took a swig, giving Jay time to catch up. "Try a mile and a half."

Reaching Frosty's side, Jay sat up on his

board. He drained his water bottle, gulping it down too fast, but unable to stop himself.

Frosty eased off his board. "Wanna paddle far, forget about the pain. Wanna hold your breath long, forget you're holding it." Setting his dive watch, he motioned for Jay to join him in the water.

As Jay slid into the ocean, Frosty continued his tutorial. "Key is to relax. Which slows the heart, allowing the mind to do what it needs to do best: absolutely nothing."

Once Frosty gave him the nod, they both submerged themselves in the ocean. Gliding effortlessly beneath Frosty, Jay released the air from his lungs. Together, the two of them descended deeper and deeper into the sea until they reached buoyancy equilibrium.

Staring into the infinite blue water that surrounded him, Jay felt a sense of utter calm overtake him. He found it both comforting and thrilling to be completely engulfed by the ocean. Meeting Frosty's eyes, he saw the same sense of peace and joy he felt reflected there.

But then the faint beep of Frosty's watch broke the stillness, and Frosty motioned him upward.

Breaking through to the surface, Jay turned to Frosty in amazement. He had spent so much time on the ocean, but had never really experienced what it was like to be beneath it before. It was an indescribable feeling.

They both gulped in air. When Frosty spoke again, all he said was, "Congratulations, Flipper— you made it all of thirty seconds."

As Frosty climbed back onto his board, Jay did the same. It didn't matter that he hadn't been down there long. That tiny glimpse of what lay beneath the waves only made him fall deeper in love with the ocean, only convinced him further that it was his one true home.

CHAPTER 7

◄ ▶

Skateboarding down the road at Capitola Mall, Jay bunny-hopped onto the sidewalk, slaloming around wandering pedestrians like they were his own personal obstacle course. As he flew past the store windows, the display at Radio Shack caught his attention. Kicking off his board, he walked closer, peering at the weather radio displayed in the window with a slew of other gadgets. It was just like Frosty's. A tag said it was on sale for eighty-nine dollars—but it might as well have been eight thousand. Every dollar he earned at Pleasure Pizza already went to helping out at home.

As he leaned in closer, he thought he saw Blond reflected in the glass, standing in the parking lot beside a black Trans Am. Spinning around, he was about to call to his friend when he saw who he was with—Sonny Purrier, semi-disguised in a stocking cap and sunglasses, leaning against the car with one of his cronies. Jay saw Blond surreptitiously stuff something into his pocket as he passed Sonny a wad of cash. He felt his stomach drop, certain that whatever his friend was up to, if it involved Sonny, it couldn't be good.

He skated over to an abandoned house where he and Blond like to hang out. It had an empty pool in the back that was perfect for skateboarding, and no one ever bothered them there. They had planned to meet up that afternoon, and he just hoped Blond would still be there.

As he vaulted over the iron fence, he saw that Blond and their friend Bells were already there. Walking across the weedy, overgrown yard, he tried to think of what to say to his friend. But as soon as he joined them, the other guys dropped into the deep end of the pool, carving from one vertical concrete face to the next, and he followed them. He noticed that Bells's arm was in a cast, but the guy didn't let that slow him down. After skating back and forth too many times to count, the three of them paused in the shallow end to catch their breath.

"Hey, so Hollybra's having a party tonight," Bells said. "You clowns going?"

"Sounds good to me," Blond agreed. "Jay?"

"Nah, man, got school and stuff tomorrow."

"We all got school," Blond protested. "That's no excuse."

"I heard that, haven't been to class all week." With that, Bells pivoted, skating hard into the deep end.

Watching their friend, Blond shook his head. "And the dude actually wonders why he's a second-year sophomore." Then he turned to Jay, scrutinizing him. "So what kind of stuff you got going?"

Jay shrugged, not sure how to answer. Frosty hadn't ever said to keep their training a secret, but he didn't think he'd like Jay advertising it, either. Especially since he *had* made Jay promise not to mention Mavericks to anyone. But he didn't want to lie to his friend. After a long moment, he said, "Just trying to make sense of everything. All the little pieces and paths, you know." He gave Blond a pointed look. "You ever been there?"

"We're in high school, man," Blond said, his tone making it clear that of course he'd been there—hadn't everyone? Jay was about to ask him about Sonny then, thinking this was as good an opening as he was going to get, but before he could, Blond took off again, speeding down the length of the empty pool.

Jay didn't follow right away, watching his friend instead. He had been friends with Blond for seven years and had never known him to get mixed up with the dealers or the junkies that hung around Pleasure Point. And Blond had always been as wary of Sonny as Jay had. Much as he wanted to ask Blond about what he'd seen, he couldn't bring himself to say the words. He wanted to help his friend, but then again, maybe it was better if he didn't know.

Covered in sweat, Frosty stood on a ladder, nailing the last corner of a tarp onto the roof of a house in Soquel. Through the treetops, he saw Jay approaching on his bike. With a glance at his watch, he smiled to himself.

Charging past Frosty's parked van, Jay maneuvered through the construction equipment and broken pieces of composite shingles that littered the driveway. "Hey, Frosty," he called.

Despite the nearly irresistible glimmer of longing in the kid's eyes, Frosty forced himself to sound tough. "You're early."

Jay looked surprised. "You said to be here at four. It's twenty to four."

"Exactly." Frosty hammered in another nail, ignoring the kid's confusion. He hated lateness, but being early could be just as inconvenient. That was one life lesson he figured the kid might as well grasp right now.

"So where's all your crew?" Jay asked, looking around.

"You're looking at it." After driving in one final nail, Frosty started down the ladder. "Chief cook and bottle washer."

He strode past Jay and began loading his equipment into the back of his van.

"So we ready?" The kid was eagerly eyeing the two paddleboards strapped to the top of the van.

"Does it look like we're ready?" Frosty gestured to the debris that covered the driveway, annoyed.

"No."

"We'll be ready once this driveway's been cleaned up." Handing Jay a shovel and a pair of work gloves, he added, "That's what you get for being twenty minutes early."

But Jay didn't seem at all bothered by being put to work. With his usual easy grin, the kid dug into the closest pile of shingles, working hard and fast. Frosty couldn't help but feel impressed.

The late-afternoon sun glimmered on the water as Frosty and Jay paddled, grinding on their knees. Pausing in his paddling to catch his breath, Frosty glided for a moment. When Jay slowed beside him, Frosty fixed him in his gaze. "Being 'exact' means no deviation. It means being precise and unyielding. And if I'm gonna teach you anything, whether it's how to survive a wave or hammer a nail, it's gonna be done with a methodology in place. Is that clear?"

"Yes, sir."

"Okay, back to baking. So we got the four pillars of a human foundation. They are: the physical, the mental, the emotional, and the spiritual . . . though I admit to being a little wobbly in that department."

"I'm not sure I understand, sir," Jay told him.

"Attaboy." Finally, Frosty gave him a smile. "Doubt and faith, chief. And let's knock off the 'sirring,' all right? You wanna show me respect, just work hard and pay attention. Besides, sirs are at least fifty anyway." His expression turned introspective as he said, "Brenda's father . . . now, *he's* a sir. Never lets you forget it, either."

Jay didn't know how to respond to this revelation, but Frosty seemed to have forgotten, for a moment, that he was even there. So Jay kept quiet, not wanting to upset his teacher by jarring him back to the present before he was ready.

As the fog began to lift, Frosty gazed toward the distant outline of the Monterey Peninsula, the lights on its shore twinkling in the dawn. "You know what a thesis is?"

The question seemed to come out of nowhere, but Jay just replied, "Um . . . an idea?"

"An idea that attempts to explain something, lays it out to be proved or disproved. So here's our thesis: It's thirty-six miles across the bay from Santa Cruz to Monterey. The day you're able to paddle it, is the day you'll be ready for Mavericks. And not a moment sooner."

"But . . . that's impossible." Staring at Monterey, far across the bay, Jay shook his head.

With a chuckle, Frosty replied, "More so than you know. Looks pleasant enough now, but once you get farther out, it becomes a minefield of wind, current, and swell—just like Mavericks. Now, paddling is all about the physical, in order to build strength and stamina. Meaning, from now on, you'll be grinding every day."

"On this?" Jay gestured to the paddleboard.

"On that," Frosty confirmed. "The mental will be tied to your own research: calculation of the tides, currents, and your ability to navigate 'em all. And the emotional pillar will ultimately play upon the demons of your own exhaustion. That clear?"

Though he was still trying to absorb everything the older man had said, Jay asked, "What about the spiritual pillar?"

"Don't have an answer for that. All I know is that's what sometimes makes the impossible *possible*." Frosty reached out his hand to Jay. "Monterey equals Mavericks. Deal?"

Eyes narrowing with determination, Jay turned his gaze from the distant peninsula and back to Frosty. Reaching out to grip the man's hand, he gave it a firm shake.

"Good. Then I'll need your mom to sign a permission slip, accepting responsibility for anything that might happen to you along the way." Dropping Jay's hand, Frosty turned his board around.

Jay stared at the surfer's back, shocked. He hadn't expected Frosty to treat this like an elementary school field trip. His mom wouldn't understand why this was something he had to do. She would just freak out and refuse to let him try. He had figured out years ago that it was easiest not to tell her what he was doing—then she couldn't worry, and she couldn't object. Since she was gone all the time anyway, it wasn't exactly hard to keep things to himself. "But . . . what if she won't sign it?"

Ignoring his question, Frosty paddled toward shore. "Deep breaths, steady rhythm, drive and glide," he called. "Stay with me now." He never looked back.

With a heavy sigh, Jay followed, doing his best to keep up. Soon, the sheer physical effort overcame his worries, leaving no room for anything but the force of his arms pushing through the water, propelling him back to the shore.

That night, the moon lit the way as Jay climbed a twisty cypress tree in front of a weathered

Nantucket-style house. It was a beautiful home, so much grander than his own beach shack, like the kind of place a real family would live. When he reached the second story, he peeked in to see Kim doing homework on her bed. As he shimmied higher up on the thick branch where he was perched, a few twigs snapped beneath his feet. Kim turned at the noise as her dog, Sophie, began to bark. The dog ran to the window and put her big paws up on the windowsill. Kim followed, pausing to wrap a kimono-like robe over her pajamas. When she opened the window, she found Jay leaning on the sill, smiling in at her.

"Sophie! Hey, girl!" he said. The dog barked once more, her tail wagging in recognition.

"Shhh!" Kim whispered, shushing both Jay and the dog. "My parents are asleep. What're you doing here?"

"Sorry." He dropped his voice to a whisper to match hers. He knew her parents had never liked her hanging around with him, and finding him at her window in the middle of the night wasn't likely to improve their opinion. "Look, could you write me a permission slip with my mom's signature? My cursive blows."

Of course there were plenty of girls in his classes who he could have asked for help, but Kim was the one he always thought of when he needed help. When they were kids, she really had been like the big sister he never had. Now—well, he wasn't sure what they were to each other. Besides, it was another excuse to talk to her, and he would take as many of those as he could get.

"A permission slip? For what?"

Looking into her clear blue eyes, the moonlight haloing her blond hair, he couldn't tell her anything but the truth. "I haven't told anyone, so you'll have to promise to keep it a secret."

She raised her eyebrows at him, and her expression so perfectly conveyed that of course he could trust her, that he immediately burst out with the rest of it. "Mavericks—it's real. Might be the biggest wave in the world. And I saw it with my own eyes, just up the coast. Frosty's gonna train me to surf it."

"Mavericks?" Now she looked at him as if he had said he'd seen Frosty surfing with a yeti. Like all the kids who grew up in Santa Cruz, they had heard the legend of Mavericks: Hawaii-size waves just off the coast, in some mysterious spot few had ever seen. Most people assumed it was a myth concocted by Santa Cruz surfers who merely dreamed of big-wave surfing on their own turf, probably when they'd had a few too many and were wishing for bigger surf. No one took it seriously.

"I swear. Like nothing you've ever seen. And if I ask my mom for permission, it'll just give her an excuse to act like a mom for once, and she'll probably say no." He desperately wanted Kim to believe him. Anytime anything important happened to him, she was the one he wanted to tell. Nothing felt quite real if she wasn't a part of it.

As this thought popped into his head, the truth of it hit him hard. He drank in the sight of her, like a princess in a tower, with her short pink robe and flowing blond tresses. He couldn't help saying, "You, um . . . look great."

She met his gaze for a moment before breaking it, suddenly shy. "Thanks." That single word contained a multitude of meanings—that she was flattered, that she was embarrassed, that he shouldn't say things like that to her.

Trying to lighten the mood, he added, "Would've asked you at school, but I know you

don't like to be seen in public with younger men."
He said it like a joke, though it really wasn't. She
did avoid him in front of her older friends.

She couldn't help but grin. "Okay, fine. So
what should this permission slip say?" Grabbing
a notebook and pen from her desk, she stood
poised, ready to take notes.

Relieved, he dictated the note to her, though
she made a few changes to make it seem more
grown-up. When it was finished, they both
agreed that it sounded like something a mom
would write. Not his mom, necessarily—but
then, Frosty didn't know his mom. Jay could only
hope it would be good enough to fool him.

When he got home with Kim's note tucked safely
in his pocket, he was so revved up he couldn't go
to bed. He veered away from the darkened back
unit that was now his own domain and into the
main bungalow. In the bathroom, he filled the tub
and even dumped in a little of his mom's bubble
bath. Then he climbed in and ducked beneath the
water, determined to practice holding his breath
longer. He couldn't embarrass himself in front of
Frosty again.

From under the water, he heard his mom shouting, "Jay, honey? I'm home. You here?" But he kept counting off the seconds anyway. If he surfaced now, he would have to start all over.

She opened the bathroom door just as he bolted upright from beneath the suds, gasping for breath as he checked his watch. "One forty-six. Almost two full minutes."

His smile faded as he took in his mom, looking frazzled in her black-and-white waitress uniform, her face contorted with fear and fury. "I thought you were drowning in there!" she shouted.

He stared at her in shock. He hadn't meant to scare her. Honestly, it had never occurred to him that she might get home from work before he went to bed anyway, much less that this little exercise might upset her.

"Hey, sorry. Just a surfing thing I'm working on."

She shook her head, throwing her hands in the air as she left the room and shut the door behind her.

He scrambled out of the tub and back into his clothes. It seemed like he was always having to comfort his mom, but he wasn't used to being the source of her anxiety. She certainly didn't need more things to worry about, and he wanted to make sure she knew she didn't have to worry about him.

CHAPTER 8

◀ ▶

Frosty sat in his van on East Cliff Drive, eyeing his house from down the block as he did on so many nights. With his seat reclined, he was absorbed in his crossword puzzle book, though he glanced up every few minutes to check on his house. When the lights in one bedroom and then another went out, he slid a bookmark into his book, snapped on his headlights, and pulled away from the curb.

Slipping quietly into the house, he found Brenda in their bathroom, getting ready for bed. "Kids asleep?" he asked, though of course he knew the answer. He always tried to stay out of the house until both Roque and Lake were down for the night.

His wife shot him a look that said she knew

exactly what he'd been doing. She usually did. But she didn't call him on it this time, and he gratefully headed for bed. Eyes closed, he felt her slip in beside him moments later.

It seemed like no time at all passed before morning. He'd gotten up before dawn, careful not to disturb his wife as he climbed out of bed and stumbled into the shower. But when he emerged from the bathroom, he saw a light emanating from the kitchen in the predawn darkness.

As he walked in, he found Brenda sitting at the kitchen table, looking through a pocket-size photo album.

"What're you doing up so early?" he asked. Figuring he might as well pack himself a lunch while they talked, he grabbed a jar of mayo from the fridge, a can of tuna from a cabinet, and a loaf of bread from the counter.

Looking up from the book, Brenda said, "Lake woke me up, and I just got him down, but I couldn't get back to sleep." She took a sip from her morning cup of tea.

As he sat down across from her to assemble his sandwich, he got a closer look at the photo album, and stiffened. He recognized it as a relic from his childhood, one he thought he had stashed away long ago. "What're you doing with that?" he asked.

"Found it in the dresser you moved into the baby's room." She smiled to herself. "You're so beautiful."

Meeting her gaze, Frosty wasn't sure whether she was talking about him or about his baby pictures. Before he could ask, she launched into a speech he could tell she had been practicing.

"Look, I know surfing's an addiction and I know it's your escape. But you can't put the rush of a thirty-foot drop in front of your two children. You of all people." She reached for him across the table, grasping his hands, not allowing him to flee as she gazed into his eyes. "And I get it, Frosty, I do."

He turned away, fighting back an unexpected rush of emotion. He didn't know if it was the sight of those old photos or her reminder of how early he had lost his parents, but he suddenly felt like he couldn't stay in that room for one more minute.

Except Brenda seemed to see that, and before he could bolt, she was out of her chair, wrapping her arms tightly around him. "You're a good man," she whispered, leaning in to rest her head on his. "But you could be a great man." Then she kissed him tenderly, lips soft and lingering, and he felt himself relax. "Just don't lie to me. Now go prepare that boy for that wave of yours."

With that, she walked out of the room, leaving him alone with his thoughts. Pushing back from the table, he noticed the photo album still lying open. Without quite meaning to, he scooped it up and stuffed it into the pocket of his jacket. After sticking the sandwich in his lunch bag, he headed out the door.

Rain pounded down on him, and he huddled in his jacket as he dashed to his van. Once inside, he clicked on the light and slipped the book from his pocket. After wiping a layer of dust from the cover, he opened it to a black-and-white picture of a towheaded four-year-old boy, laughing as he hung from his father's neck in a backyard pool. Frosty smiled, remembering—not that moment specifically, but the feeling of happiness and safety he'd had with his dad, and never since.

He felt like that little boy again as he gazed at an image of himself in a suit, standing between his mother and father on the steps of a church. "Rick's First Communion, 1955," his mother had written across the border at the bottom of the photograph. It had been years since anyone called him Rick. Smiling, he turned the page and found the next one blank. Clenching his jaw, he kept flipping pages, but every one was empty, the memories cut off abruptly.

Bundled in his hoodie, Jay stood in his kitchen, wolfing down a banana while strapping his wetsuit onto his backpack. After tossing the banana peel in the trash, he headed for the front door.

But as he passed his mother's room, he stopped short. Seeing that his mom was still huddled under the covers, he threw open the door and flipped on the light.

"Mom, what're you doing? You have a six o'clock shift. You wanna lose another job?" Dashing for the bathroom to get the shower going for her, he paused to stash his backpack and wetsuit beneath the couch. He counted on her being gone for work before he left to meet Frosty so he wouldn't have to field any questions about where he was going.

Once he heard his mom close the bathroom door, he filled the coffeemaker with water and turned it on. Squinting down the street toward the rain-streaked window, he tried to make out Frosty's van. When he glanced at the clock and saw it read 6:26, he felt his frustration building to a boil.

"Come on, Mom, let's go! Hurry up!" he shouted.

"Hold your horses, I'm coming," she muttered, shuffling into the front room in the white blouse and black vest she wore for her waitressing job. She paused to corral her hair into a ponytail before grabbing her purple purse and keys from the table by the door.

"Have a good day," he told her. He watched anxiously through the window as she climbed into her station wagon and backed out of the driveway. Once she was gone, he sprinted for the door, grabbing his backpack on the way.

Sprinting through the rain, he spotted Frosty's van waiting at the curb. He yanked open the door and dived inside just as Frosty reached across to stash a photo album in the glove compartment.

Glancing at the clock, Frosty announced, "You're eleven minutes late." He slammed the glove box closed, locking away whatever was inside.

"I know, sorry," Jay replied, flustered. "My

mom, she, um . . . had to sign my permission slip." He didn't know why, but he didn't want Frosty to know how hard he had to work to keep his mom on a schedule. Instead of explaining that, he pulled a folded piece of paper out of his backpack and handed it to the other man. Then Jay had to look away, fumbling in his bag as though searching for something really important, afraid Frosty would immediately recognize the permission slip as a fake.

But all Frosty said was, "Your mother's got nice handwriting. She take much convincing?"

Jay looked up, shocked. "No, not too much."

With a nod, Frosty tucked the paper in his pocket. As Frosty headed north on Highway 1, Jay tried to hide his relief. Frosty seemed to know everything, so it was hard to believe he had pulled one over on the older surfer.

Frosty's windshield wipers squeaked as they battled the rain. Gazing out at the farmland that flashed by outside his window, Jay pulled a tinfoil ball from him backpack. He unwrapped a smashed chocolate cupcake and started stuffing pieces of it in his mouth.

Suddenly, Frosty reached over and snatched it out of his hand. "You're actually eating this for breakfast?" he demanded.

"Yeah." Jay shrugged. He always just grabbed whatever he could find at home, and it wasn't like there was ever much to choose from.

Shaking his head, Frosty balled up the tinfoil around the cupcake and chucked it into the back of the van. They drove on in silence, Jay feeling both embarrassed at getting caught eating that junk and frustrated that now he had nothing at all to eat. He tried to ignore the gnawing feeling in his stomach, but Frosty must have heard it rumbling.

Reaching into his lunch bag, Frosty pulled out a tuna sandwich and set it on the dashboard in front of Jay. "Here."

Jay hesitated. Despite his hunger, he didn't want to eat his teacher's lunch.

"Go on, take it," Frosty insisted, and Jay waited only an instant longer before he obeyed. Ripping open the Ziploc bag, he devoured the sandwich.

"Gonna need it more than me today," Frosty said, as though justifying his actions to himself. Jay nodded gratefully as he chewed.

Frosty reached over and turned on his shortwave radio. "Winds out of the northwest at twenty to twenty-five knots," the recorded voice said. "Buoys reporting six feet at eight seconds westerly at two hundred forty degrees."

"Weather radio, huh?" Jay asked, glad to have something to break the silence.

"That's the NOAA—National Oceanic and Atmospheric Administration," Frosty explained. "They've got buoys and satellites measuring every weather front on the planet. Storm chasers use 'em to track hurricanes and tornadoes."

"And you use it to track big surf?"

"That's right." Frosty seemed to be finished talking, but once Jay finished off the sandwich, he strove to keep the conversation going.

"So how come you call surfing the sport of kings, anyway?" he asked. Frosty shot him a suspicious look, but Jay met his gaze with clear-eyed earnestness.

"Surfing comes from Hawaii, where it was the sport of royalty. But I don't use that term for *surfing*. Given time, anyone can learn to surf. But big-wave riding is something you're graced with. And if you're given that gift . . . you answer the call."

Jay nodded, feeling the weight of Frosty's words. The big-wave riding he had seen Frosty and his friends do was nothing short of miraculous. He could only hope that he had the gift, too.

The wind continued driving the rain at them as they parked at Montara State Beach. The two men suited up and carried their boards down a trail cut into the high grass. Below, Jay saw windswept sand and whitecapped seas. Rounding the bluff, he saw the crushing waves stacking up and breaking all along their lengths in a massive detonation of whitewater.

"Closing out big-time," Jay said.

"Yep." Frosty's tone made it clear that this was so obvious, it wasn't even worth saying.

But Jay had a point to make. Eyes on the storm-filled surf as they continued their march down the path, Jay explained, "I mean, there's no way to get out there. Especially on a longboard."

Turning, Frosty gave him a long look. "Oh, there's a way, all right. So let's see if you're worth your salt, chief."

As the wind slashed rain against his face and waves pounded the shore, Jay pulled up the hood of his wetsuit and nodded. Running against the force of the wind, he raced down the trail to the shore and threw himself into the churning surf. Battling the water, he tried to force the nose of his board beneath the shore break, but it pounded him backward into the shallows. After several more failed attempts, he realized he was being sucked far down the stormy coastline in a rip current.

Glancing farther up the bluffs, he saw Frosty smiling wryly down at him. Jay dived in once more, only to be swept down the beach again, a mere speck in the foaming waves that carried him to shore.

Lying splayed in the sand, Jay heard Frosty whistling "The Lion Sleeps Tonight" as he walked down the beach toward him. "Back to baking," Frosty told him. "Follow me." Jay struggled to his feet and staggered along behind.

"You didn't even make it out thirty yards," Frosty shouted over the roar of the wind, rain, and sea. "Keep in mind you gotta get through more than half a mile of that just to get in position at Mavericks. You gotta conserve all of the energy you can. So, let's take a look at what you missed. For some reason, you decided to paddle straight out. But take a look at the rocks over there. See what's happening to the current?"

Watching the relentless current swirling around the jagged rocks, Jay saw exactly what

Frosty meant. "It's—it's got nowhere to go."

"Nowhere to go but where?"

"Back out to sea?" Although he could see that this was true, Jay felt tentative after his recent failure.

"Exactly! To the casual observer, it's a swirling pool of water. But to a waterman, it's a conveyor belt." Pulling up his hood, Frosty raced to the waterline, hurling himself into the ocean and paddling alongside the rocks. As the current swept him out to sea, he turned back to Jay with a smirk and a shrug, his point made.

Smiling, Jay jumped in at the same spot and followed the other surfer out into the ocean. It was amazingly easy now that he was working with the current instead of against it.

They paddled back to shore, side by side. As they climbed back up the hill toward the van, Frosty said, "Today's lesson was about the power of observation. Simple fact is, you got two choices. You can fight things head-on, or you can observe the laws of nature." Frosty stopped walking to fix Jay with his intense stare. "Because if you look hard enough, there's always a way through it. Make sense?" When Jay nodded, Frosty started walking again.

"Good. 'Cuz you're gonna write me an essay on it. Three pages, typewritten, single-spaced. Devil's in the details of whatever you observe. And I'll expect it by week's end."

Jay's eyes narrowed with confusion. How was writing an essay going to help him become a better surfer? This wasn't what he thought he had signed on for, but he knew better than to argue. After all, he had promised he wouldn't.

After a long shift at Pleasure Pizza, Jay rode his bike across the dead front lawn of his bungalow. Dismounting, he locked his front wheel to one of the rusty porch railings before heading inside.

In the silence of the dimly lit kitchen, Jay stood at the counter, counting out the night's tips. He sorted his dollar bills into various envelopes— one for the phone bill, another for the electric company, another for their water. When he had added enough cash to each to cover the bills for another month, he walked back outside, still wearing his stained Pleasure Pizza uniform.

In the back unit, he pulled out the cigar box where he kept his most important possessions.

First he removed a Radio Shack ad for a weather radio, just like the one he had seen at the store. Next he retrieved his savings from the box and began counting it. But as he counted, he couldn't resist looking at the letter from his father, buried beneath a bunch of coupons he had saved for shops on the boardwalk. Without wanting to, he picked up the letter, transfixed by the power it still held over him. Flipping it over to avoid seeing his father's name, he stared at the sealed envelope for a long moment. It didn't matter what was inside—he would still blame his father for leaving. Maybe that was why he kept it, to remind him of the anger and pain that would never go away. He honestly didn't know why he hadn't just chucked it years ago. Shoving it back into the box, he piled his savings on top of it and shut the lid.

Grabbing his sticker-covered notebook, he flipped to a blank page and began to write. He had to record Frosty's words before he forgot them. *"The fact is, you got two choices,"* he scribbled. *"You can fight things head-on, or you can observe the laws of nature. Because if you look hard enough, there's always a way through it."* He thought that just might have been the most valuable advice he had ever gotten, and he wanted to make sure he could always refer back to it, no matter what.

CHAPTER 9

◀ ▶

Students sprawled out on the grass outside Soquel High School, soaking up the sun on their lunch hour. Off by himself, Jay leaned over his open notebook, brow furrowed in concentration as he wrote "Power of Observation" across the top of the page.

Looking up, he saw Kim and her girlfriends across the lawn, talking to that delinquent Sonny and his crew of older surfers. Behind his shades, Sonny looked remote as they all laughed and flirted. Kim used to know better than to hang around punks like Sonny, but it seemed all that had changed once she hit high school. Although he wasn't even sure Sonny was still in high school—he had certainly never seen that guy in a classroom. But Jay was sick of thinking about

Sonny, worrying about him. Turning his attention back to Kim, he studied her from afar, writing as fast as he could.

When the bell rang signaling the end of lunch, Sonny and his crew took off, while Kim and her giggling friends sauntered inside. Jay trailed after them, trying to write and walk at the same time. After bumping into a couple of other students on his way back to the building, he gave up. He had already lost sight of Kim in the crowd anyway.

The rest of the day passed in a blur. Every spare moment he got, Jay flipped open his notebook to his essay, reading it over, crossing things out and writing in better details. He hoped his teachers wouldn't notice that he was less attentive than usual, but honestly, Frosty's essay was more important to him than anything he was learning in school. He liked school fine, and he wanted to do well, but his training with Frosty was his life.

Once the school day finally ended, Jay hurried outside and grabbed his bike. Dodging cars and students as he ran the gauntlet of campus traffic, he heard someone honking and calling his name. He looked up to see Kim pulling up beside him in a convertible black Jeep Wrangler, its top down to let in the sunshine.

"Need a lift?" she asked with a grin.

"Um, sure. Thanks." Caught off guard, Jay fumbled his bike into the back of the Jeep and hopped in. Once he was seated, Kim gunned it down the road, blaring "Round Here" by the Counting Crows on her stereo.

"Nice ride," Jay said. He hadn't even known she had a car.

"Actually more of a bribe. My parents subscribe to the theory of operant conditioning. So it's on lease. I get one C and it's history. Below a thousand on my SATs, gone." Bitterness tinged her voice as she added, "Which is why I've got SAT prep class every day, three to five."

Trying to be supportive, Jay said, "Sounds fun."

Kim shook her head "Chinese water torture. And today's September seventh, which only adds insult to injury."

Staring at her, Jay tried to puzzle out the significance of the date. He knew it wasn't her birthday, and he couldn't think of any holiday that fell on September 7. After a moment, he gave up. "And that would be why?"

"Because seven is in the house of Libra," she explained, her tone matter-of-fact. "And being that I'm a Libra, it's supposed to be an auspicious day, astrologically speaking."

Jay didn't know much about all that astrology stuff, but he nodded anyway. "So why don't you bail on it today and help me use these up instead?" He pulled a handful of coupons from his pocket, brandishing them like a wad of cash.

When she glanced over at him, she had to laugh. "Are those funnel cake coupons?"

Grinning back, Jay just shrugged. "Hey, what's one day? Astrologically speaking."

A smile spread across her face. She swerved into a U-turn, heading for the boardwalk. They lucked out with a close parking spot and walked together along the shore, Jay wheeling his bike beside him. The ocean was flat and shiny as glass as they made their way down the boardwalk.

When they reached the funnel cake stand, he whipped out his coupons, enjoying the gallantry of being able to treat. They both ordered apple funnel cakes and stuffed big gooey pieces into their mouths as they strolled.

"First day we moved to Santa Cruz, my mom took me down here. Got all-day wristbands and she bought me a Slush Puppy, with one of those crazy straws. And the very first ride I made her take me on was *that* one." Jay pointed up at the Giant Dipper, a wooden roller coaster that was the centerpiece of the beach boardwalk, towering high into the sky.

"No—the Giant Dipper?" She paused to shoot him a wide-eyed look. "You weren't even big enough, were you?"

Holding his thumb and forefinger just the slightest bit apart, he said, "Barely squeaked through. I took one ride, and that was it—I wouldn't get off it for the rest of the day."

Kim laughed, the sound so light and pure that Jay immediately tried to think of ways to make her laugh again. "And what about your mom?"

"Um, I think she was good for maybe five, six loops. After that she sat on a bench and just waved as she watched me go on it, over and over." He smiled, remembering the sheer joy of that day.

"A little boy's dream, I guess." They tossed their plates into a trash can as they passed, not minding the stickiness of their fingers.

"One of the best days of my life. Looking down, seeing her sitting there, smiling. Like she was gonna stay happy forever." He trailed off, and Kim gave him a look that seemed to see deep inside him.

"Any word from your dad?"

He shook his head, suddenly uncomfortable in his own skin. To change the mood, he swung his leg over his bike and said, "Hey, hop up. I'll take you on a poor man's log ride. C'mon." He patted the handlebars, and she tentatively climbed on.

Jay peddled along the waterline, faster and faster, listening to the water lapping at the shore. Kim giggled and squealed with the thrill. "I'm almost afraid to ask, but—how is this a poor man's log ride?"

With a Cheshire grin, Jay swerved into the foamy waves. Kim shrieked as the thick spray of water splattered them. They both laughed uncontrollably as they barreled down the beach.

When they reached the base of the pier, they dismounted. Leaning against the wooden pilings, they sunned themselves on the sand.

Reflexively, Jay pulled out his notebook, wanting to capture this day forever.

"Can I see?" Kim held out her hand. Even though Jay had never let anyone see his sketches, he couldn't think of a way to say no to her. So he handed it over, and waited nervously as she thumbed through the pages.

"Jay, these are amazing." Relieved, he leaned in to see her looking at the drawing of Frosty riding the giant wave.

"That's it." He pointed to the wave. "Mavericks."

"No way. It can't be that big."

He shrugged, letting his silence speak for him.

Sitting up straighter, Kim stared at him. Her stricken expression made it clear that she believed him. "Then you're insane. Are you insane?"

He wanted to explain to her why he had to ride those waves, that it was something he knew he was meant to do. But before he could find the words, she flipped to a page filled with writing.

"'Power of Observation,'" she read, and he immediately tried to snatch the notebook from her hands.

"That's nothing. Here, give it back." But she grasped his wrist to hold him off, while keeping the notebook out of his reach in her other hand.

"'From a distance I watched,'" she read aloud, "'and realized that along with rare beauty, comes constant scrutiny, like being the lead in a school play.'" Looking up from the page to see his cheeks red with embarrassment, she asked, "What, are you stalking someone?"

Refusing to answer, Jay lunged for the notebook and grabbed hold of its edge. But Kim held tight, and they rolled over each other, tumbling across the sand in a fit of laughter. They paused, faces inches apart, their laughter fading as they gazed into each other's eyes.

"I, uh . . . better get home." Kim hopped up, and Jay watched her go, all the promise of the moment fizzling out. The sudden awkwardness between them kept him from even asking for a ride back.

Once she was out of sight, Jay brushed the sand from his jeans and climbed on his bike. As he rode home, he replayed the past few hours in his mind. Despite its end, the afternoon had been nearly perfect. He hadn't felt that close to Kim in years. He hadn't realized how much he had missed her. Speeding home, he wondered when he would get to spend time with her again. She was always so busy with all her older friends, he was amazed he had gotten her to himself for a whole afternoon. And yet, it wasn't nearly enough—anything short of spending every day

.with her, he was sure, wouldn't be enough.

When he got home, he found it empty as usual. He wolfed down dinner from a tin can in the kitchen before retreating to the back unit. There, he pulled out his notebook once more, settled in at his desk with his old typewriter, and started typing up his essay for Frosty. The typewriter's ribbon needed changing before he had gotten very far, and he kept yanking out whole pages in frustration at how the words were coming out. His typing was slow, the hunt-and-peck style that his keyboarding teacher had tried and failed to guide him away from. By the time he was finished, his clock read 11:46. He had to meet Frosty at dawn again tomorrow, and he had been working on the essay so long that all the words were blurring together. Deciding it would have to be good enough, he collapsed on his bed and fell almost instantly asleep.

CHAPTER 10

◀ ▶

Jay awoke early to grind out some push-ups before he had to meet Frosty. "Twenty-eight, twenty-nine," he chanted as his mom appeared in the living room. She stood in the doorway in her pink fuzzy robe, staring at him blearily.

"Thirty, thirty-one, thirty-two." Never pausing in his exercise routine, he added, "Coffee's ready, and your uniform's hanging in the bathroom. Thirty-six . . ."

"You gonna tell me what this is about?" his mom interrupted, pouring herself a cup of coffee.

"Four pillars . . . of a solid human foundation," he explained between reps. "Forty-one, forty-two . . ."

Christy stared at him, completely lost. He thought about telling her more, but then he caught sight of the clock on the wall and jumped up. "Gotta run." With that, he darted out the door while his mom watched him go in drowsy confusion.

After school and work, Jay biked over to Frosty's and pressed the doorbell. When Frosty answered, Jay held three typewritten sheets of paper out to him. But his excitement faded almost as soon as he was face-to-face with Frosty, and all he said was, "I, um, finished the essay."

"Congratulations." Frosty remained expressionless. "You eaten?"

Timidly, Jay shook his head. When Frosty motioned him inside, he followed with his head lowered.

When they reached the kitchen, Brenda was shredding pieces of chicken before feeding them to Lake in his highchair. Frosty set out an extra plate for Jay, and he piled it high with food. Jay shoveled it into his mouth as fast as he could. He noticed nine-year-old Roque watching him and smiled at her in between bites. She blushed, ducking her head to hide behind her long, light-brown hair.

Meanwhile, he kept sneaking glances at

Frosty, who sat at the head of the table, glasses low on his nose as he read the essay. Finally, Frosty looked up. "What is this, some sort of joke?" he asked.

Jay stopped chewing, meeting his mentor's stony gaze. "No, sir."

"So lemme get this straight—I tell you to write an essay, and you observe a girl?"

Jay swallowed hard. "You never told me what to observe."

"C'mon. I mean, do I really need to, Jay?" Frosty shook his head, disgusted. "I'm training you to survive Mavericks, not some teen crush."

"I just thought—" Jay began, but Frosty slammed the pages against the table, stopping him.

With the tension rising, Brenda turned to Roque, pointed to her daughter's room, and mouthed, "Bed. Now."

Roque rose from the table with an exaggerated sigh. Wrapping her arms around Frosty's neck, she leaned in and gave him a peck on the cheek. But Frosty's eyes never left Jay, though he reached back to give Roque a pat on the back. Then she pivoted and darted toward her room, pausing in the hallway to get one last look at Jay.

Now, though, he was too anxious to give her a smile. He had worked so hard on that essay—it had never occurred to him that Frosty wouldn't like it.

Once she was gone, Frosty demanded, "You just thought what?"

"Nothing." Jay dropped his gaze.

"Well, if you didn't think, you know what? You're wasting my time." He rose from the table, anger radiating from him in waves.

"Frosty!" Brenda's voice was a reprimand, but it didn't stop her husband.

"And that's not something I have a lot to spare these days," he finished before stalking out of the room.

Setting down his fork, Jay stared at his nearly empty plate, fighting back the tears that stung his eyes.

"Excuse us, Jay." The kindness in Brenda's tone was a salve to his pain, but it made him feel even more like crying. Anyway, what really mattered was Frosty's approval, and he was afraid he had lost that for good.

Brenda hurried after Frosty. As soon as she was out of sight, Lake held up a big chunk of chicken and started to cry.

At a loss, Jay rushed over to the baby, shredding the chicken and trying to feed it to him like he had seen Brenda doing. When that didn't work, he tried to distract Lake with a game of peek-a-boo, then a sippy cup of milk. The boy continued to wail, and finally, at a loss, Jay scooped him up. Instantly, the crying stopped. Jay smiled with relief, happily cradling the baby, bouncing him and murmuring, "That's a good boy."

Sitting on his bed, Frosty removed his glasses and rubbed his eyes as Brenda closed the door behind her.

"For heaven's sake, Frosty. Not everyone sees the world through your eyes. He chose to examine something that meant the world to him, something *personal*, which he opened up and shared with you. Entrusted to you."

"I'm not concerned with his *feelings*, I'm concerned with the *objective*. The point of writing an essay is to be able to put a thought down on paper, see the gaps, and reflect." He felt sure he was right, but he found himself unable to meet his wife's eyes.

"And did he accomplish that or not?"

Frosty shook his head, regret overtaking him.

"I can't do this, all right? I only know what I know, my old man never even—"

"Shhhhhhhh. Everything you need is right here." Reaching out, she laid her hand on his heart. "It's not something that needs to be taught. It just takes patience. You owe yourself that much."

Before he could reply, she stepped back, gazing anxiously toward the kitchen.

"What is it?" he asked, standing up.

"Lake . . . I don't hear him." She yanked open their bedroom door and rushed into the kitchen, Frosty close behind.

They both stopped in their tracks at the sight of Jay holding Lake to his chest, bouncing him gently. Noticing them in the doorway, Jay explained, "Just needed to be held, I think."

Brenda shot Frosty a meaningful look. "Don't we all." Reaching out to take the baby from Jay, she added, "Thank you, sweetie."

Frosty nodded, his wife's point taken. "All right, chief, sit down." They sat across from each other at the small round kitchen table, elbows resting on the blue plaid tablecloth as they both leaned forward. Jay met Frosty's eyes with an expression of total innocence as he hung on his surfing instructor's words. "Not sure how it works in your school, but in mine, you didn't pass wood shop for doing correct algebra equations. So from here on out, let's stick to the subject at hand. All right?"

When Jay nodded, Frosty grabbed a red pen from the counter and scrawled, "DO OVER!" across the top of the essay. Sliding it back to Jay, he added, "First off, you're gonna rewrite this essay. And observe an actual break. As in *surf break*."

"And second?" Jay asked, eyes never leaving Frosty's.

Frosty picked up a half-eaten chicken leg from his plate, brandishing it. "We're gonna start working on these."

Jay's mouth curved into a curious smile, and Frosty gave him the tiniest smile in return.

CHAPTER 11

◀ ▶

Jay's legs churned like eggbeaters in the deep end of the outdoor pool at the Spa Fitness gym. Arms raised, he treaded water with a folding chair held above his head. He struggled to keep his face out of the water, sputtering as he sank below the surface.

"I'm . . . swallowing . . . water," he gasped.

Without looking up from his watch, Frosty replied, "Then you better grow gills, 'cuz you got two more minutes."

Although every second was a struggle, Jay didn't give up. Somehow, he kept both his face and the chair out of the water until Frosty said he could stop.

As Jay climbed out of the pool, Frosty said

something Jay had never expected to hear from him. "Let's go have some fun."

It was early evening when they pulled up at Bean Hollow State Beach. Jay had insisted they stop by Kim's to invite her, too, though he hadn't expected her to say yes. She had, though, grabbing a sweatshirt and jumping into Frosty's van.

Brenda was already there with Roque, while Lake dozed in his infant car seat. Their neighbor, Zeuf, and Melia, another nurse at the hospital, sat on blankets around a little bonfire, strumming ukuleles and sipping wine.

Frosty handed Jay a spearlike contraption he had brought from his van. "Know how to use one of these?"

Jay shook his head. "Don't even know what that is."

"It's a Hawaiian sling," Frosty explained. "Basically a bow and arrow for the water."

"Never did much archery," Jay replied, his eyes wandering to Kim, who was taking her place with the women around the fire.

"Ever spearfish?" Frosty noticed the direction of the boy's gaze, and hardened his voice to get his attention back.

"Sure." That was the answer Frosty had expected. It was a good skill for a poor kid who lived near the ocean to have.

"Good. You use it like you were spearfishing, only it's got more power behind it. Hoping you can manage it, 'cuz we're depending on you to catch our dinner."

With a little salute, Jay ran for the water, diving beneath the thick kelp beds that covered the water's surface. As Frosty watched from the shoreline, sipping a beer Brenda had handed him, Jay burst back out and ducked back under again, clearly taking his task seriously. Behind him, bonfires flickered all along the beach, and ukuleles and bongos echoed through the dusk.

"Seven to you, Bren," Zeuf was saying as Frosty approached their fire.

"I can do it in seven," Brenda said confidently.

Zeuf gave Melia a nod, and her friend finger-picked seven notes on her uke. "All right, name it," Zeuf said when Melia was finished.

"Oh, shoot!" Brenda stared thoughtfully into the distance, humming the notes back to herself. "I know this. Ummm . . . 'Sugar Bear.' Or, 'Honey Bear'? No, no, no, 'Honey Baby' . . . 'Honey Baby'!"

"She got it." Melia said with a grin.

"Yes!" Brenda leapt up and did a little victory dance.

Zeuf and Melia strummed the rest of "Honey Baby" on their ukes, singing along.

As she swayed to the Hawaiian tune, Brenda spotted Frosty and rushed over to grab his hand. "Get over here and sing to me, husband of mine." Taking in the sultry swing of her hips, Frosty had to smile. "Or I'll have to settle for a dance." She twirled herself into his arms, and they slow danced in the sand, her long skirt swirling around them, the fire glowing warm on their cheeks.

As they moved to the music, their eyes met, sending an electric current through him that reminded Frosty of how he had felt right before a first kiss. Leaning in, he kissed her long and hard, not caring that their friends and kids were watching. When he pulled away, he saw Roque looking at them with a bright smile on her face. As they spun, he noticed Kim gazing up at them enviously.

When the song ended, Frosty dipped his wife nearly to the sand, his love for her welling up in him. Of course he always loved her, but after two kids and so many years of marriage, it wasn't all romantic sunset dances on the beach. But this moment felt perfect, and he was glad to have it. As their friends burst into applause, he smiled sheepishly. "That's all I got for ya, girls."

He turned to see Jay surface once more, now with a big black sea bass wriggling on the end of his spear. Smiling, Frosty thought that the kid was a natural. As the kid struggled to bring the massive fish to shore, Frosty said, "Jay just speared us a fat one for dinner. Gonna scavenge us some wood."

Just like that, the moment had passed. Zeuf and Melia got to their feet as Frosty began scouting for driftwood.

"You're gonna stay for some fish, right?" Brenda asked.

"Nah, have to take a rain check," Zeuf replied. "The swing shift calls." She and Melia grabbed their gear, gave good-bye hugs and kisses all around, and headed for their car. Brenda watched her friends go, talking and giggling as they made their way across the sand.

"Why don't you go give your dad a hand?" Brenda murmured to Roque.

Eagerly, their daughter darted over to him, tugging his arm from his pocket so she could take hold of his hand. Even though that made it harder to gather wood, he squeezed her hand in return. Brenda smiled at the sight of the two of them together.

Filling her wineglass, Brenda turned to Kim with a sigh. "He used to sing to me when we'd go camping in Hawaii, which I always thought was so beautiful."

Kim smiled at this declaration. "Where'd you two meet?"

"You're looking at it. Matter of fact, this is where he took me on our first date. Asked me to dinner and the next thing I know, he's spearing a fish and cooking it over a fire like a caveman." Brenda broke into a laugh. "And I'm sitting there in my white taffeta dress and pearls, wondering where my cutlery is."

Kim giggled softly as Brenda shook her head at the memory. "Of course, being from the other coast, I thought all California nights were like this. Then the fog rolled in and I found myself freezing in the middle of summer and I realized, hmm, I've been hoodwinked." Lake stirred, and Brenda reached out automatically to rock him in his seat.

"You don't think he would have moved for

you? I mean to be with you? Or is all his family out here?"

"No, we're his only family. Frosty lost both his folks at a young age." She gazed off at Frosty and Roque, slowly making their way down the beach.

"I'm sorry, I had no idea." Kim's blue eyes flickered with sadness in the light of the fire.

"Keeps it to himself, always has. But somehow he got it in his head that it makes him unfit." It didn't make sense—after all, it wasn't like his parents had left him on purpose, or like he'd had anything to do with their deaths. Maybe it was just so many years of relying only on himself that made it hard for him to connect, or a fear of losing someone else he loved so fiercely that made him hold himself back. She dropped her voice to a whisper to add, "That's the part that breaks my heart."

Gazing across the beach, she saw Jay lugging a huge fish across the sand, a huge grin on his face. The sight of him made her smile, too.

"So tell me." Brenda turned back to Kim. "What do all his surf buddies think about what he's doing?"

"He hasn't told 'em." Kim shrugged. "Says it's kinda like not saying anything after you blow out the candles on your birthday cake."

Brenda smiled, knowing the feeling exactly. "You take care of that boy, you hear?"

"I will," Kim replied. But then she shook her head, seeming to suddenly hear what she had said. "I mean, we're just friends. But . . ."

Before she could finish, Jay finally reached them, brandishing the huge sea bass on his spear. "All right, who wants to kiss a fish?" Dripping wet, a grin stretching from ear to ear, he hoisted the sea bass toward them.

"Don't get that near me, Jay, I swear—" Kim shrieked, laughing as she ran away from him. Jay chased her down the beach while Brenda watched, eyes misty with nostalgia. Young love always got to her, but these two especially: a talented young surfer and the good girl who didn't even know she had already fallen for him.

Jay Moriarity (Jonny Weston)

▲ Surfers at Mavericks

▲ Frosty Hesson
(Gerard Butler)

Jay's mom, Christy
(Elisabeth Shue) ▶

▼ A memorial for Jay

◀ Jay and Kim
(Leven Rambin)

Jay getting ready
to surf ▶

▼ Jay skating

▲ Frosty

▲ ▼ Jay and Frosty

Surfer at Mavericks, off the coast
of Half Moon Bay, California

CHAPTER 12

◀ ▶

As she entered her house the next afternoon, Brenda was stopped short by the blare of a skill saw and an air compressor coming from her kitchen. Peering around the corner, she saw that her kitchen had been turned into a construction zone. A tarp covered the floor while Frosty cut wood trim on a circular saw. Jay stood on a stepladder, blowing sawdust from the newly refurbished cabinets.

"Hey," she said, still trying to make sense of the scene.

Startled, Frosty turned toward her. He scrambled to shut down the compressor with his foot while pulling off a surgical mask that shielded his mouth from all the dust. Jay froze, too, the kitchen suddenly draped in silence.

"Hey . . ." Frosty looked like a teenager who had been caught sneaking out.

"What're you two up to?" She included them both in her smile, wondering why they looked so guilty about what appeared to be a much-needed kitchen remodel.

"Ah . . . had some extra scrap wood. Thought we'd fix the place up a bit. Jay and I . . ." Frosty's eyes darted around the kitchen as though searching for someone else to explain things to her. "It's not done yet."

"Hmmmm . . ." She stifled a laugh at his statement of the obvious.

"Frosty wanted to surprise you," Jay added. Frosty glared at him, but Brenda thought it was sweet of the boy to want to chime in like that.

Taking in the new cabinet doors and freshly painted walls, she shook her head in amazement. Even half finished, it was obvious that they were building her a dream kitchen.

Seeing that Frosty didn't want to meet her gaze, she realized that he wasn't doing this just because he felt like it—he was doing it as penance for something. Looking at the kid helping him, it all clicked: Frosty was remodeling her kitchen to make up for surfing Mavericks when he had sworn he wouldn't. Never mind that he could have simply apologized and then not surfed those monster waves again. Frosty wasn't good with words, but he was good with his hands. He was building her an apology.

"He continues to surprise me," she said. Not wanting to embarrass him in front of the kid, she resisted the urge to run to her husband and kiss him. Sweaty and covered in dust, he still looked awfully sweet to her. With a brisk nod, she said, "Carry on, then," before making herself scarce. Behind her, after a pause, she heard the sounds of construction resume.

Jay flicked off the storefront lights of Pleasure Pizza. Making his way to the back, he tossed his apron into a hamper and grabbed his bike. As he wheeled it out the back door, he saw Blond down at the far end of the alley, leaning into the black Trans Am Jay had seen at the mall. The alley was deserted otherwise, all the shops opposite already closed. Blond's hair gleamed under the flickering fluorescent lights that lent the scene a sickly glow.

While he watched, Blond handed Sonny some cash and received a small paper bag in return.

Lounging in the backseat, Sonny counted out the money. Glancing up, he noticed Jay watching them. Shooting a mocking smile at Blond, he said, "Looks like Little Trash's keeping tabs on you."

Blond strode toward Jay across the pavement, with a smirk that matched Sonny's, his chest puffed out and his walk a swagger. His every movement and expression seemed calculated to prove that he didn't care what anyone thought of him. But Jay knew he did care, about his opinion at least—he knew that was why Blond had been hiding this from him. Blocking the door with his bike, Jay fixed his friend with a disapproving look.

"What's this, man?" Blond demanded, flashing a sharkish smile. "You, like, all of a sudden the narc squad?"

"You having this conversation with me or your conscience, Blond? 'Cuz all I wanted to tell you was it's your turn to lock up." Pulling a set of keys from his pocket, Jay tossed them to Blond, who caught them automatically. Then Jay swung his leg over his bike and rode off without a backward glance.

Bubbling with anger, Jay blasted through the

back alleys, racing from one block to the next. As he cut over to the main drag, something caught his eye. Veering into the parking lot, he braked suddenly, meaning to stop beside Kim's Jeep but fishtailing into a wipeout in front of her instead.

Startled, she rolled down her window. "You all right? What're you doing?"

He leapt to his feet, brushing himself off, trying to act unfazed. "Just got off work. You know, spinning pies, living the dream." He smiled, his fury over the Blond situation melting away at the sight of her. "You?"

She nodded to the Spa Fitness building behind her. "Was hoping to go for a swim. But I guess they close early on Sundays."

"You wanna swim at night, you gotta use the back entrance." When she gave him a questioning look, he smiled bigger. "Hop on, I'll show you."

She got out of the car and climbed up onto Jay's handlebars, a grin spreading across her face as they wove down the sidewalk. He couldn't stop smiling, either, at the thrill of having her this close.

Kim squealed as Jay zigzagged down the alley, finally braking alongside a twelve-foot brick wall. "Don't tell me this is the back entrance," she exclaimed.

Hopping atop the Dumpster, he extended his hand to her. "It's the unofficial back entrance. Don't worry, we do it all the time." Once he had hoisted her up, Jay scaled a telephone pole. He looked back to see Kim shaking her head, but she followed him anyway. He couldn't help pausing to watch, impressed at her climbing skills. When he reached the second story, he leapt onto the roof, then reached out to help Kim join him.

She hesitated before following him across the gravel rooftop, stopping short when she caught sight of the dark pool below. The outdoor pool was bordered by the roof on all sides, but stood open to the night air in the center of the courtyard. "So wait, how do you get down to the pool?"

"Only one way I know of," he replied, already pulling off his red Pleasure Pizza shirt. He mimed a dive.

"You're joking, right?" She sounded nervous, but he just gave her a playful grin.

Raising her eyebrows, she snuck behind an air-conditioning unit to slip out of her jeans and T-shirt. Jay couldn't resist glancing over, catching a flash of arm or leg, luminous in the moonlight.

"Hey," a voice called, and they both jumped.

Spinning around, they saw Blond leaping onto the roof from the telephone pole. Jay wasn't exactly thrilled to see his friend. For one thing, he had wanted some alone time with Kim. For another, he was still angry, and still didn't know what to say to Blond. But it wasn't like he could ask the other guy to leave. After all, like the abandoned house where they skated, this was a spot the two of them had discovered together.

As he headed toward them, Blond said, "Saw your bike, you didn't tell me—" It occurred to Jay then that his friend had been looking for him, maybe hoping to patch things up.

Seeing Kim standing there in her bikini, Blond stopped short. She reflexively held her T-shirt up to her chest, covering herself.

Blond stared for a moment longer before turning to Jay. "So does she understand the rules?"

Kim gave Jay a questioning look as Blond stripped down to swim trunks, his thin body pale in the moonlight. "It's kinda like figure skating— points based on a combination of style, execution, and difficulty."

Kicking off his shoes, Blond headed to the edge of the roof. "For example, I'm gonna start with a standing one and a half. High, I repeat *high*, level of difficulty, because I gotta clear the pool deck. Hit that, you're immediately disqualified." Blond closed his eyes, arms outstretched in front of him.

Concerned, Kim leaned over and whispered to Jay, "He's not serious, is he?"

Before Jay could answer, Blond somersaulted off the roof, disappearing from sight. A moment later, a thundering splash echoed up to the roof. Shocked, Kim raced to the ledge. Looking down, she saw Blond, bobbing to the surface with his fists raised in triumph.

"And judges say?" he shouted up to them.

"Are you outta your mind?" Kim demanded, her voice pitched high with worry.

"Not bad, Blondie." Turning to Kim, Jay added, "He pretty much nailed that. And just so you know, the only thing that can trump it is a reverse back layout. 'Cuz of the blind entry." Keeping his eyes fixed on the ledge, Jay backed up across the roof.

"I can't watch this." Kim covered her eyes. "This is insane."

"You have to. You're the only judge." With that, Jay charged for the ledge and leaped off, arching backward. Then he tucked his knees in and rotated, landing in the pool with a perfect cannonball.

As he surfaced, Jay grinned up at Kim. While she stared at him, speechless, Blond cheered raucously.

"And the crowd goes wild!" Blond exclaimed. "The competitors neck and neck as the judge tallies the scores!"

Kim couldn't help but laugh, adding her applause to Blond's.

Gazing up at her, silhouetted against the night sky, Jay was swept away by her beauty. Glancing at Blond, he noticed that his friend was looking at her the same way. But before he could react, Kim leapt off the roof with a piercing battle cry. Sailing through the air, she hit the pool with an explosion of turquoise water, landing between the two boys as they cheered her on. Laughing hysterically, she burst back to the surface, thrusting her arms into the air in victory. "And the judge-turned-competitor ties Moriarity in the final round." She swam to the side and announced, "Coming down to a final sprint, to see who the real champion will be."

Grinning at the challenge, Jay paddled toward

the edge of the pool, but she lunged forward before he reached the side. "And they're off!" she shouted. Although he spun in mid-stride, she was already two lengths ahead.

Swimming fast after her, he ducked under-water, moving effortlessly through the pool. He surfaced, laughing, and saw her looking back at him, her gaze flitting over his broad shoulders and sinewy muscles. He couldn't help feeling pleased at the admiration he was certain he saw in her eyes. Then he ducked under again, reaching out one long arm to grab her by the ankle, yanking her back and touching the far wall first. They both broke the surface of the water in unison, sputtering with laughter.

"He cheated!" Kim cried. "Moriarity is DQed!"

"No, there's different rules here." Grinning, he splashed her playfully. "You can only win if you're Jay."

At that, she leapt atop him, giggling as she shoved him underwater. As he sputtered back to the surface, he noticed Blond, silently treading water at the far end of the pool, no longer laughing with them. He looked so lonely there that Jay started to swim toward him, but suddenly Kim attacked him with a huge splash of water. He whirled to retaliate, and soon they were in a full-on splash fight. "A little backup?" he shouted to Blond, trying to include him, but his friend shook his head.

"I think you got this." Blond climbed out of the pool. "I need to get outta here anyway."

Jay wanted to go after his friend, but he couldn't tear himself away from Kim, not when she was laughing and hanging off him, the proximity of her breathtaking beauty overwhelming him. Nights like this didn't come along often, and he wasn't going to let it slip away. So he turned back to her, telling himself he would have plenty of time to fix things with Blond later.

CHAPTER 13

◀ ▶

The next morning, Jay skateboarded down Soquel High Road toward his school. Hitting the timer on his wristwatch, he inhaled deeply and held his breath. He flew past students toting book bags, a homeless man sleeping in a box at the side of the road, and even Blond and Bells, hooky-bobbing from the bumper of a school bus on their skateboards. He waved, and Bells waved enthusiastically back, while Blond simply gave him a nod as they passed. They would have to talk things out, and soon. Neck veins bulging, he checked his watch: 1:52, 1:53, 1:54 . . . Stepping off his board, he paused to gasp for air.

As he regained his breath, he saw Kim's black Wrangler pulling into the parking lot. He was about to wave when he saw two older surfers climbing out after her. His eyes narrowing with hurt, Jay turned away. It looked like the previous night hadn't meant nearly as much to her as it had to him. He had to keep reminding himself that they were just friends, that she saw him more as a kid brother than boyfriend material. Suddenly, he didn't feel like going to biology class anymore. He just wanted to be alone.

Pivoting, he skateboarded back the way he had come, and held out his thumb on the main road. Soon a farm truck stopped, its bed crowded with migrant farmworkers.

"Where you headed?" the driver asked.

Without planning it, Jay replied, "Pillar Point."

The man nodded. "Get in the back."

As the truck rumbled north on Highway 1, Jay huddled with the others in the back, bracing against the cold wind. The ocean thundered beyond the farmsteads that lined the highway.

When the truck swerved over to the side of the road, Jay leapt out, shouting his thanks as the driver pulled back out again.

Jay headed up the dirt path toward Pillar Point, carrying his skateboard and backpack. Up ahead, he saw a lone truck parked in the tall weeds, and wondered whose it was. Not many people knew about this place, so it was almost certainly one of Frosty's friends.

Listening to the distinctive booming of Mavericks in the distance, he made his way up the cliff. At the top, storm clouds hovered over the ominous satellite dishes. He shimmied around the barbwire, heading toward the beckoning tempo of the break. He hadn't brought his board, and wouldn't have dared to face those waves without Frosty yet anyway, but just being near them made him instantly feel more at peace.

Below, he spotted a surfer he recognized as Jeff Clark, one of the first to ever surf Mavericks, and one of the men he had seen with Frosty. The waves rolled beneath him like mountains as the man faced the stormy surf alone.

Sitting on the bluff, Jay unzipped his backpack and removed his notebook. The howling wind blew across his face as he took in the elements, jotting down questions for himself: *Tide? Swell? Rip? Entry? Exit?* These were things he needed to know about if he were going to ride these monsters. Now was as good a time as any to start taking notes on what he saw below.

Suddenly, he saw a dark rogue set on the

horizon, and stood up to watch as the surfer paddled for the choppy peak. The man paddled hard, digging deep, until a treacherous wave caught him. It sucked from beneath him, pitching him from his board and skipping him like a stone across the wave's face. Finally, the vicious tonnage of water overcame him, throttling him as the whitewater exploded. Jay stared in disbelief as the wave seemed to bury the man alive.

Jay sprinted down the bluff, straining to find the man amid the black churn. But as the massive waves relentlessly broke and exploded, the surfer remained hidden from view. As Jay drew closer, he spotted a dark form clinging to the edge of a jagged rock that jutted out of a pit swirling with the spume of backwash. He exhaled a breath he hadn't realized he was holding. The surfer was alive.

He helped Jeff back to shore, and found him surprisingly calm. "That's Mavericks, man," he explained as dried off on the sand. After taking a moment to catch his breath, he headed back up the cliff, Jay following close behind in case the surfer needed any help.

When they reached his truck, the man offered Jay a ride home, and Jay gratefully accepted. He hadn't really thought about how he would get back from Pillar Point. Jay could hardly speak on the ride home, too shaken by what he had seen. Jeff knew Mavericks better than anyone, and if even he could be taken out by it—well, that meant no one was safe.

Jeff let him out at his house, calling, "Tell Frosty I said hey, okay?" before pulling away.

While the surfer had seemed to take his near-drowning in stride, Jay was fighting not to freak out. Of course he had known surfing Mavericks was dangerous, but it hadn't really hit him *how* dangerous it was until he witnessed the older man's near-death experience.

Jay realized then that he was going to need to know a lot more before he faced those waves. Grabbing his bike from the backyard, he took off again, for the library this time.

That night, Jay pored over an array of coastal maps from the library books stacked all over his room. With careful concentration, he drew the ocean topography beneath Pillar Point, adding detailed notes on the reef formation beneath Mavericks.

On the opposite page, he sketched a surreal

scene of a man being pulled deep underwater by lashing tentacles. The sound of muffled screams echoed in his head, though in truth the man hadn't even had time to scream before he was yanked under.

Even after he tucked the notebook beneath his pillow, he couldn't keep the scene from replaying in his mind. For a few horrible moments, he had been absolutely certain that he had just witnessed a man being killed by the waves. He couldn't sleep, tossing and turning for hours. Finally, he gave up trying, sitting up to read the surfing books he had checked out, flipping through them until he finally passed out near dawn.

He barely had time to sleep before he had to wake up for school. When his alarm went off, he dashed for the shower, throwing on clothes and racing out the door. He wanted to talk to Frosty before school, and he was already running late.

Racing his bike past Frosty's driveway, Jay found it piled with broken pieces of composite shingle. Up on the roof, a shirtless Frosty used a roofing shovel to chisel off the old shingles.

As he paused to catch his breath, Frosty spotted Jay below. "And to what do I owe this honor?" he asked.

"Um . . . was just wondering." Looking up, Jay shielded his eyes against the bright afternoon sun. "Why do they call it Mavericks, anyway?"

Squatting down, Frosty paused to take a long drink from a can of soda before answering. "After an old German shepherd who liked to swim in the bay. Dead now."

Jay looked at him questioningly, but Frosty just shrugged. "Just a dog that swam out with the first surfers who went there. They didn't surf the big waves, and the dog seemed to have the most fun of the bunch, so they named it after him. Never said it made a lot of sense."

Laughing, Jay replied, "Good thing his name wasn't Fluffy. Doesn't have quite the same ring to it." He was relieved when Frosty laughed, too, and figured that would be a good time to ask a more serious question. "Would you ever surf it alone?"

"Depends on how good it was." Frosty turned his attention back to the roof, ripping another old shingle free.

"What if something happened out there? I mean, and there was no one around to help?" He decided not to tell Frosty he had been out there yesterday, had seen Jeff Clark almost drown, even though that was the reason he was asking.

"Why you think we're doing all this? Something happens out there, the only one who can help you, is *you*." Locking eyes with Jay, he recited, "'The surf rider must take care of himself. No matter how many others are with him, he cannot depend on any of them for aide.'"

"You say that now, but—" Jay began, but Frosty stopped him.

"I didn't, Jack London did. And if the guy who wrote *Sea Wolf* said it, it's good as gospel." Giving Jay a half smile, he tossed the empty soda can down to him. Jay caught it easily. "Now get outta here. I got work to do."

As usual, Jay didn't argue, just hopped back on his bike and rode to school. But as he did, the Jack London quote echoed in his head. Somehow, he had thought that training with Frosty would mean that his mentor would help him when he actually faced the big waves. But of course that was impossible. Once you were out there, it was just you and the waves. That was what he loved about surfing—but with waves as big as Mavericks, it was a terrifying thought, too.

CHAPTER 14

◀ ▶

The next afternoon, Jay rode up to the Hesson place again. Stopping at the mailbox, he slipped a folded essay inside.

Brenda watched him from the top of the driveway, where she and Zeuf were unloading rosebushes from a wooden flat. "So tell me, how's it all going?" she called down to him.

Taking in her curious expression, Jay suppressed a laugh. "Definitely keeping me on my toes."

"Not too hard on you, is he?" She gave him a warm smile, but honestly, she worried. She knew how Frosty could get, and strong as this boy was, she could see that he was sensitive, too.

"Nah, sometimes I kinda feel it's the other way around."

"How's that?" Setting down a rosebush, she

looked at him more closely.

He met her eyes with a frank expression. "If you've been through a lot in life and stuff, sometimes you're hardest on yourself. I mean, that's the way it is with my mom at least."

"Sure you're only in high school?" she asked, shaking her head at his insight.

The two shared a smile before Jay took off, Brenda fondly watching him go.

"That kid's got some good intuition, no denying it," she said to Zeuf, eyes never leaving Jay as he rode out of sight. Seemed to her that a boy like that could only be a good influence on her husband.

Spectators and surfers crowded the parking lot of the lighthouse at Steamer Lane, pouring toward the cliffs overlooking Santa Cruz's most popular break. Climbing over the safety rail with his board, Jay strapped on his leash and made his way toward the narrow promontory of the cliff, eyes never wavering from the ten-foot surf that had drawn the crowd. Partway down the cliff, he found Blond, sitting beside his board as he watched the heavy sets roll in.

"Hey," Jay said awkwardly. They still hadn't

talked, and he knew it would only get harder to break the silence the longer it went on. "You going out?"

Blond wouldn't even look at him. "Like you care." Jay drew back, startled and unsure of what to say.

But Blond wasn't paying attention to him, anyway. His eyes were locked on an incoming set. "Outside!" he shouted, and now Jay saw that he was calling to Sonny, out in the water.

Sonny raced for the wave, but another surfer got there first. Catching the peak, the surfer slipped to his feet. Undeterred, Sonny spun and dropped in in front of the other man, forcing the other surfer into the crushing lip, where he was taken out. Cranking a bottom turn, Sonny whipped off the vertical face, dissecting the wave in a flourish of spray as he charged down the line. He clearly had surfing skills, but no surf etiquette, which was essential, too.

"Boy can get it done," Blond muttered, shaking his head in admiration.

"If that's what you call snaking someone's wave, you're right." Jay wasn't going to stand there and listen to his friend idolizing a punk like Sonny.

But as he turned to leave, Blond snapped, "Guess we can't all be as perfect as you, can we, Jay?"

Voice calm and gaze piercing, Jay faced his friend. "You're my best friend, Blond. You really think I don't get what you're doing with Sonny and those guys? You're better than that."

Walking back toward his friend, Jay reached out his hand and smiled, trying to breach the gulf between them. "Now let's get back to basics and go get some."

Softening, Blond grabbed Jay's hand and let himself be pulled to his feet. The two hustled down the narrow promontory of the cliff together. But suddenly, Jay picked up his pace, racing faster and faster before launching himself off the side of the cliff. Tightly gripping his board's rails, Jay sailed airborne as if floating on a single wing of a plane, before plummeting into the ocean twenty-five feet below.

Surfacing, Jay grinned up at Blond, who was gazing at him with a mixture of jealousy and pride. "You coming?" he shouted.

Blond hesitated. "Um . . . go ahead, man."

Nodding, Jay turned and paddled for the outside as a large set built on the horizon. He thought he had seen apprehension on his friend's face, but it was hard to know from down here. As a twelve footer loomed, he wondered if he should have insisted that his friend join him. But then, surfing when you were having an off day was never a good idea. Before he could think about it too much, the pack of surfers charged for the peak like a flock of seagulls converging on raw bait.

Racing the pack, Jay's paddling strength allowed him to reach the peak first. As the peak feathered, Jay dropped into the wave of the day. He bottom turned and tucked into the slot, carving down the line as the entire lineup watched in awe. Harnessing the wave in an array of fluid cutbacks, Jay ejected off the back in an airborne crescendo.

Up on the cliff, Blond howled for his friend, grinning from ear to ear. Jay even caught Sonny glancing back at him, an expression of grudging admiration on his face.

As the next wave approached, Jay whipped around his board, coming face-to-face with the younger surfer Sonny had cheated out of the wave. "All yours, man," Jay told him. Jay had already ridden his own wave, after all. "Go, go, go!"

The younger surfer beamed as he dug into the wave. Jay cheered him on as the kid rocketed down the line, more of Frosty's advice echoing in his mind. *"The simple act of giving away that which is coveted is inconceivable to most. Then again, few can understand what it feels like to walk on the moon, fall through space, or ride a great wave. There are certain experiences in this life that are revealed only by the experience itself."*

Just then, something made him look up at the cliff. There, against the safety rail, among the crowd, he spotted Frosty. The older man gave him a nod and half smile before walking back toward his van. But that was all the approval Jay needed.

Later that night, Sonny and his crew stumbled into Pleasure Pizza, drenched from the rain outside and as high as kites.

Behind the counter, Jay and Blond turned as Sonny teetered up to them, hoodie pulled low, eyes unfocused. "Gimme a hot dog. Extra chili," he demanded. "Check that. Make it a jelly doughnut."

Blond and Jay exchanged a leery glance. "All we got is pizza, bro," Jay told him.

Sonny looked up, taking a beat to steady himself. "Hey, Little Trash, I know you. Look at that drum. Why you smiling all the time, huh?"

As a nervous smile sprang to Jay's lips, Sonny glowered. "There it goes again. See, when you smile, you look like a little wuss. And when you look like a little wuss, you get no respect."

Sliding a pizza into the oven, Blond muttered just loud enough for Jay to hear, "Sure got it today, pinhead."

But Sonny heard him anyway, flying over the counter and seizing Blond by the throat. As Sonny slammed his friend to the floor, Jay dove between them. An uncontrollable fury overtook him as he grabbed Sonny and cocked back a fist.

"Let go of him! Now!" Jay shouted, struggling to free Blond from the punk's grasp.

Sonny's crew yanked Jay back, hollering for Sonny to chill. Sonny finally released Blond, who coughed for air, grabbing at his throat.

Shaking off his crew, Sonny growled, "Throw a punch, better pray I never get back up, you little punk. Think you're better than the rest of us, don't you? I seen you paddling out there with Frosty every morning."

Still rubbing his throat, Blond shot Jay a

surprised glance. Jay ducked his head—he hadn't wanted Blond to find out about his training like this. He also didn't like the thought of Sonny spying on his training sessions.

Barking out a threatening laugh, Sonny asked, "So what is it, Little Trash? You looking for some kind of medal, or just a chest to pin it on?" Jay fumed, taking that for a reference to his missing military dad—though with Sonny as high as he was, who knew if he had thought through the insult that well.

"C'mon, man, let's get outta here," one of Sonny's buddies insisted, tugging him toward the door. As they pulled him out into the rain, Sonny shouted, "Paddle, paddle, paddle, little grom."

Standing motionless, Jay grimaced at the term for a little kid surfer. Staring at Blond's feet, he spotted a thick roll of cash tied with a rubber band. "Think you dropped something."

Blond bent down to grab the cash and shoved it into his pocket. Jay glared after him as Blond stormed into the kitchen. Maybe he was hiding things from Blond, but clearly his friend was hiding things, too. And at least what Jay was doing wasn't illegal.

They managed not to speak for the next hour,

helping customers and making pizzas without even looking directly at each other. It was only when they were cleaning up at the end of the night that Blond finally broke the silence.

"So what'd he mean?" As he wiped down tables, Blond watched Jay sweeping up. "About paddling and all that."

Jay continued sweeping, not answering, so Blond kept talking. "Remember when me and my cousin jacked that motorcycle from the Boardwalk. Hid it up in woods near Felton. I didn't tell a soul except you."

"It's not like that, Blond." Jay finally stopped sweeping to look at his friend.

"So then what *is* it like?" Blond asked.

Seeing the concern in his friend's eyes, Jay softened. But he couldn't resist saying pointedly, "Don't worry, nothing to do with stealing or dealing." He immediately saw that his words had stung.

Tossing the cleaning rag onto a table, Blond replied, "Guess everyone's gotta do what they gotta do. And I gotta bounce. I put your tip money in the jar. *You* lock up tonight."

As Jay watched Blond head for the back room, he felt guilt gnawing at him. Guilt for not telling his friend about Frosty and Mavericks. Guilt for making accusations instead of coming out and asking Blond what he was doing, and why. He knew Blond would never have turned to dealing if he weren't desperate. Blond had been his first friend in the surfing community, and Jay would always be grateful to him for that. He knew he had to find a way to make things right.

CHAPTER 15

◀ ▶

An early mist rose with the sun, fields still wet from the night's rain. Frosty's van sped north on Highway 1, the Pacific Ocean shimmering in the distance.

Lost in thought, Jay gazed out the window. Pulling the rewritten essay from his coat pocket, Frosty tossed it on the console.

After eyeing it for a long moment, Jay swallowed hard. "So, um, what'd you think?" He had turned his notes from his morning alone at Mavericks into a new "Power of Observation" essay, and he thought it was pretty good. Then again, he had thought the last version was good, too.

Eyes fixed on the road, Frosty replied, "I think that's what I expected from you all along.

You done good, chief."

Jay beamed as Frosty turned to give him a wink and a smile. "Now, what do you say we turn those observations upside down?"

This time when they reached Pillar Point, Frosty asked his friend Frank to take them out on his fishing boat. Once they had climbed aboard, the boat's engine roared to life. As Frank piloted through the channel, Jay watched a flock of pelicans dive-bomb the glassy waters. Sitting on the stern, Frosty and Jay pulled on their wetsuits and fins.

"That'll do, Frank! Anchor here!" Frosty had to shout over the noise of the engine, but the fisherman did as he said.

Eyeing the break, Jay was surprised to see Mavericks unrecognizably flat.

"Now, the lion sleeps," Frosty explained. "But when she's breaking, you're gonna hear it from a mile away. From a half mile away, she's registering on the Richter scale. And sitting out here . . . no words can describe what you're gonna feel." Pointing north, Frosty continued, "The wave breaks right there, where the reef drops from forty to fifteen hundred feet."

Jay stared at him, trying to imagine a drop-off of that magnitude.

"Here's what you want to avoid: that crop of rocks there, we call 'the bone yard.'" Frosty indicated a jagged outcropping of rocks. "And 'the pit,' which is the impact zone in this area here, where the waves detonate one right after another." He pointed again, and Jay recognized the spot where he had seen Jeff Clark get stranded. "But the major wrath of Mavericks is 'the cauldron,' which lies at the other end of the reef here. You get sucked over that ledge and the undertow gets ahold of you, you're guaranteed a two-wave hold-down." In a voice so soft he seemed to be talking to himself, he added, "That's if she lets you up at all."

So intent on Frosty that he almost forgot to breathe, Jay struggled to tamp down the fear he felt at the older surfer's words.

"So the key is, you need to put yourself in the right position. Meaning you have to triangulate." He pointed up to the middle satellite dish on the bluff. "See the biggest dish up there?"

When Jay nodded, Frosty continued. "Think of yourself as being at the apex of a triangle. Draw a line between yourself, that dish, and the mushroom rock over there." He pointed south to a big rock shaped like a mushroom. Jay recognized it as the one he'd watched Jeff cling to for his life.

"Too far inside, you're sucked into the pit. So like the air force says, 'Aim high.'" Pulling on his mask, Frosty said, "Now let's see what makes her tick." He set his dive watch and flipped back into the water with a splash.

Jay pulled on his own mask and followed Frosty. The two of them glided down forty feet to where shafts of sunlight revealed a proscenium of jagged stone. Pockmarked with sharp crevices, the reef was as foreboding as the prodigious waves it created. Schools of brightly colored fish darted past as they continued along the contours of the reef. It ended abruptly, and Jay and Frosty peered out over the edge, staring down into the abyss. The two hung there motionless for what seemed an eternity.

Jay watched curiously from behind his faceplate as Frosty bent his pinky down alongside his ring finger, just as his watch began to beep. The two made eye contact, and Frosty pointed to the surface. They ascended together, toward the prisms of light glinting through the water's surface above.

But suddenly, a large shadow eclipsed the sunlight. Jay's gaze shot skyward to see the unmistakable outline of a great white shark winding ever so slowly through the water. The prehistoric creature loomed above them, as big as a car.

Jay froze, eyes wild and unblinking. Frosty tapped his shoulder, but Jay didn't react. Grabbing him, Frosty pulled him away from the passing shark. Eyes still locked on the menacing silhouette, Jay remained motionless.

Frosty dragged him to the surface, swimming quickly to the boat's swim step. Face ashen, Jay ripped off his mask and scrambled aboard.

As he turned, he saw Frank on the upper deck, brandishing a twelve-gauge shotgun. "Don't worry, I got your backs." Frank chambered a round, but the shark kept swimming, so he didn't have to shoot.

Hands trembling, Jay struggled to regain his breath. "Must've been twelve feet, that thing . . ."

"More like fifteen," Frosty replied. "Whole section of coast down to Ano is a breeding ground. You all right?" When Jay mustered a nod, Frosty continued, "You panicked down there. What happened?"

"I saw a fifteen-foot shark—what do you mean, *what happened*?" Jay threw up his hands in disbelief.

"And I'm sure that scared the living piss outta you, but that wasn't my question. Why'd you panic?"

Jay shrugged. "Fear, I guess."

"One thing you gotta know—fear and panic are two separate emotions. Fear's healthy. Panic's deadly." He motioned out toward Mavericks. "'Cuz when this place is firing—and I mean, thirty-, forty-foot waves—it's all about *fear*. But you *panic* out there, like you just did? You die." With that, he called to the fisherman, "Let's take her back, Frank!"

The boat engine fired up, and Frosty took a seat on the gunwale. After a moment, Jay sat down beside him.

Jay was shaken by Frosty's words, but not ready to let the issue drop. "I mean, if you're scared to death, how do you *not* panic?"

"By identifying the fear, and why you're afraid. Not just out there, but in life. Acknowledging it, so you're not paralyzed by it." Frosty grinned, clearly struck by an idea. "Welcome to your next essay."

In between school and work and training sessions, Jay helped Frosty finish his kitchen remodel. Not that he really had the time to spare, but he was honored that Frosty wanted his help, and after everything the man had done for him, he couldn't imagine saying no. Together, they hung the cabinets, laid the Spanish tile, and fitted the butcher-block counters. As a roofer, Frosty knew all the suppliers and got good deals on the materials. He had a clear vision for the kitchen, but Brenda soon got in on the act, flipping through tile samples and showing them her favorites. Since it was supposed to be Brenda's dream kitchen, Frosty always listened, trying to give her exactly what she wanted. For Jay, it was amazing to see how love could be demonstrated through something as seemingly mundane as a remodeling project. He felt like he should be taking notes on their relationship, just like he did on surfing, in case he ever got a chance to apply those lessons to Kim.

It was wonderful, too, to feel like a part of the Hesson family, to be welcomed into their home, which was so much more appealing than his own lonely bungalow, and to their dinner table to share their home-cooked meals. He liked gaining Frosty's appreciation, and earning Brenda's warm smiles. He even liked helping out with the baby and chatting with Roque. With each day he spent there, he felt more like part of the family. It was a feeling he wasn't used to, a feeling he didn't want to let go.

Soon, he realized that this work was helping his training, too. His once-slender arms and shoulders were becoming increasingly defined with each task he completed. He felt himself growing stronger. More important, he felt the glow of Frosty's approval as he helped create the kitchen of Brenda's dreams.

He enjoyed the tangible results of this work, too. Seeing the particle-board cabinet doors transformed with their new, shiny oak facing, seeing the cracked linoleum floor and countertop made beautiful with patterned tile and polished wood, he felt such a sense of accomplishment. Surfing was amazing, but it was all in the moment, over so quickly. What they were building here was something that would last, a place where this family would gather and be nourished for years to come. He loved the thought of that.

CHAPTER 16

◀ ▶

"November 19th, 1994—Paddled 22 miles round—"
Jay was writing in his notebook, adding to his
surfing log, when he heard a tapping at his door.

Looking up, he saw his mom sticking her
head in. "Hey there," she said.

"Morning. Your uniform's in the dryer." He
turned back to his notebook, assuming that was
all she had wanted.

"I know, I saw. Thanks, honey." Realizing
she was still hovering in the doorway, he looked
up again. "I was wondering if—" She hesitated,
an embarrassed expression on her face. "If you
wouldn't mind lending me fifteen dollars. Got
another parking ticket. You know, and if I don't
pay it . . ." Her voice trailed off.

Jay couldn't say no to her, not when she

needed his help. "Sure," he agreed. Grabbing his cigar box, he removed the shortwave radio ad and pulled a twenty-dollar bill from beneath it.

As he handed her the money, she said, "I'll pay you back, I promise."

He nodded, knowing she wouldn't. She never had before.

Drawing in a shaky breath, she added, "And it looks like we're gonna have to rent this back out, baby. Just not making ends meet, you know."

He just stared at her until she left. He couldn't imagine going back to camping out in the living room, protecting his mom from loser tenants. Slowly rolling up his remaining cash, he thought what a joke it was compared to Blond's thick roll. He sank to the floor, deflated. He was already working whenever he wasn't in school or surfing. He couldn't think of any way to earn more than he already did. No way was he giving up his training for more shifts at the pizza place—but he couldn't handle having no place to call his own again.

Sitting in his biology classroom, Jay stared at the wall clock, not even noticing the Thanksgiving decorations all around it. He guessed the holiday must be getting close, but it didn't matter much when you didn't have a family. Holding his breath, he watched each second ticking past. When the second hand hit the twelve, Jay added a third stroke to the top of his paper. The teacher droned on at the blackboard, but it was all white noise to Jay. Neck veins bulging, eyelids fluttering, he remained determined to make it a few more seconds before drawing a breath.

Next thing he knew, a girl was shaking him awake. He lay in the aisle by his desk, apparently having pushed himself too far and passed out. Again.

"There you are," the girl said with a giggle. Looking up, he saw that the whole class was staring. With a shrug, he hefted himself off the floor. He had still managed to hold his breath for more than three minutes. Not long enough, but it was progress.

With his classmates still watching and laughing at his wipeout, he gave them a little bow, earning a round of applause. He figured it was always better to be in on the joke than to be the butt of it.

In the Pleasure Pizza parking lot that night, Jay hefted trash bags into the Dumpster, wet sludge dripping from the bags and down his arms. As he wiped it off on a rag from the restaurant, he gazed up at the full moon. Turning back toward the door, he saw a familiar black Trans Am parked across the street, Sonny sitting on the hood in his black stocking cap.

Looking from Pleasure Pizza to the dealer, Jay teetered in a moment of indecision. It would be so easy to get some extra cash the way Blond did. The junkies were going to buy from someone, after all.

But before he could do something stupid, a cavalcade of beach cruisers blew down 41st Avenue. A flock of teens zoomed past, their bikes loaded down with coolers.

A bell jingled, and Kim veered away from the pack and over to Jay. "Hey. Was hoping I'd see you. We're doing a bonfire down at the cove. You wanna come down after work?"

"Thanks, but—" Jay began, but one of the teen's shouts cut him off.

"I wanna fry, time to get high!" the guy exclaimed as he flew by. Kim couldn't help but snicker. But Jay wasn't exactly in the mood to hang around with that crowd.

Gazing at her in the moonlight, Jay said,

"C'mon. I got a better idea."

Jay raced back into Pleasure Pizza, past Blond leaning on the counter, apathetically taking an order over the phone. "Blondie, I gotta bail early tonight," Jay called from the back room.

"How early's early?" Blond called back. When he saw Jay wheeling his bike out, Blond cupped his hand over the phone, exasperated. "Dude, it's not even nine."

Jay gestured to the nearly empty restaurant, but Blond wasn't paying attention. He was looking at Kim, leaning against the front window.

"C'mon, Blond, gimme a break. It's important. I'll owe you for life."

"You already do," Blond muttered resentfully, clenching his fists. Returning to his phone call, he said, "Yeah, yeah, half Hawaiian and half Santa Barbara, no spinach, I got it." Covering the receiver again, he glared at Jay. "Whatever, go, get outta here. And take your friggin'—" but Jay was out the door before he could finish.

It wasn't until he and Kim were almost to his house that he realized he had left his notebook behind. Much as he wanted to think that Blond wouldn't look in it, with the way they had left things tonight, he knew he couldn't count on that. But he pushed the thought away. He wasn't going to let anything ruin the evening he had just lucked into with Kim.

When they reached his place, he quickly changed into his wetsuit while she waited outside. He grabbed his longboard—Kim's was already strapped to her bike. They biked over to the Pleasure Point Ravine. When they arrived, he nimbly navigated the riverbed as he led the way to the ocean, Kim following behind with her board tucked under her arm.

"Take it this isn't your first time here," she said.

"First time with anyone else. Always kept it to myself." The truth was, this had always been his most treasured spot, his inner sanctum, and he had never wanted to share it with anyone else. But as he watched her soaking in the beauty of this place, he knew bringing her here had been the right choice.

When they reached the beach, she set down her board, staring awestruck out at the dark ocean. Breathing in the stillness of the night sky, Jay pointed to a brilliant star on the horizon. "See that? The seventh-brightest star in the sky, Rigel. And directly above it, on either side there, are Betelgeuse and Bellatrix. The shoulders of Orion."

Their eyes met, Kim's expression turning serious.

"What?" he asked.

"How do you know that?" She tilted her head back, gazing at the glimmering stars.

"From, ah . . . my dad. Started teaching me about the stars when I was maybe four or five. Had this telescope that we'd take out on clear nights. Just me and him." He tried to never think about his dad, but when he did, he mostly just felt angry at him for leaving. This was one of the few good memories he had of his father, and he felt it sweeping over him like a tide, threatening to drown him. "There's eighty-eight constellations, but . . . never got a chance to learn 'em all."

He felt Kim looking at him, absorbing his words, but he couldn't meet her eyes. Saying that aloud had brought the pain too close to the surface, and he didn't know what would happen if he let it out.

But then she laid her hand on his shoulder and said, in a voice full of understanding, "Might be time to learn the rest."

He turned to her, feeling closer to her than

ever before, and laid his hand over hers. "You still believe certain things are written in the stars?"

Her face lit up. "I can't believe you remember that. And yeah, I still do. What about you?"

He shrugged. "I read somewhere that fate doesn't just happen, but plays a part, depending on a person's actions. Which always seemed to make sense. As far as stars being aligned and all that."

Anxiety flickered across her face, but she held his gaze. "And what if they aren't? Aligned, I mean. Then what?"

He didn't know what to say. It seemed like there were so many obstacles between them—he was too young and poor for her, she was too pretty and popular for him. And yet—here they were, together again. Something kept drawing her back to him, despite their differences, and it gave him hope that maybe one day their stars would align. After a long moment, she broke the silence that hovered between them. "You do know who Orion was, don't you?" she asked.

This was part of what his father had taught him, and Jay remembered every word. "He was the Warrior. Son of the sea god, Poseidon, who taught him to walk on the waves. When Orion died, he was so beloved they added him to the heavens."

Fixated on the sky, Jay took in the majesty of the night sky over the ocean, so deep and dark but flecked with light. "Not a bad place to wind up."

Their eyes met with a magnetic intensity, as though sharing a secret through their look, and Kim smiled, her expression tender in the moonlight.

Grabbing her hand, he pulled her toward the water. "C'mon, let's go."

The two of them raced into the shallows, diving atop their boards as they paddled out into the glassy darkness. They stroked in unison toward a welling peak.

"All yours," he murmured. Sliding to the tail, Kim pivoted her board around. She sprang to her feet and made the drop, sweeping across the shoulder-high, moonlit wave.

"And mine." She spun to see him dropping into the same wave, and burst out laughing. Speeding alongside her, Jay cross-stepped down his board, then leapt onto the back of hers. His hands on her waist, he steered her down the wave. Kim and Jay both exploded with laughter as they rode tandem, moving as one with the wave.

As they neared the shore, their soft laughter echoing across the ocean, he thought he saw someone watching them from the cliff. He picked out a familiar flash of blond hair in the moonlight before Blond pulled up his hoodie and rode off on his bike. Maybe it hadn't been his friend—it was hard to see in the dark, and at this distance. Before he could think about it too much, he and Kim were back on the beach, flushed and giggly and running together across the sand. He didn't think he had ever had a night this perfect. He never wanted it to end.

CHAPTER 17

◀ ▶

Drenched in sweat, Jay and Frosty paddled side by side across Monterey Bay, their powerful strokes as perfectly matched as those of seasoned oarsmen.

"When we dove Mavericks, you were keeping track of time on your fingers." Jay spoke in rhythm with his strokes.

"Yep." Frosty glanced over at him. "Ever black out from holding your breath too long?"

"No . . ." Jay lied.

"Well, you do it underwater, it'll be your last." Frosty's voice was steady, matter-of-fact. "The longer you're down, the more your mind unspools. The more it unspools, the less present you are. Been under there times when I don't even hear my watch alarm."

"So I don't get it. What do you do?"

"You don't rely on your watch, and you stay present by counting to yourself. And every sixty seconds you notate it with one of your fingers. Run outta fingers, you know you're in trouble." Sitting up as he drifted to a stop, Frosty turned toward Jay. "You feel it getting colder? That's because of what's beneath us—"

"The Monterey Trench." Frosty looked surprised at the interruption. "Five thousand, two hundred and eighty feet deep. Current drops in here, heads east until it hits the southern wall," Jay said.

"Oh yeah?" Eyebrows raised, Frosty gave him a half smile. " Creating what?"

"A back eddy," Jay said confidently.

"So then you know the day we hit that eddy is the day we push the limit. And you're gonna feel the limit pushing right back. You'll be more tired than you've ever been. But we'll also be more than halfway across the bay, which means for the first time, we'll be closer to what's in front of us than what's behind." His speech finished, he turned to look at Jay curiously. "Where'd you learn all that?"

"From you," Jay explained. "I mean, in books and maps. You told me to study the tides and currents."

A proud smile on his face, Frosty met his eyes. "Guess I did, didn't I?"

Frosty stared down into the dark-green surface of the deep. "I used to paddle out here to the deepest point, and bob like a cork. Just to *feel* it."

He seemed completely absorbed in his memories now, and Jay tried to call him back. "Feel what?"

"That's for another day, chief," Frosty replied, almost too low for Jay to hear. Shaking it off, he turned his board around.

Jay paddled after him, still pondering the older man's words. He thought he understood. After all, that was why he liked to go out on the water alone at night—to feel the power of the sea all around him, to put his problems into perspective against the great expanse of the ocean. That was the feeling that had made him fall in love with surfing.

Late that afternoon, Frosty stood on the shoreline of Pillar Point with his three surfing buddies beside him, motionless as they stared out at the pounding surf. It seemed they stood there forever, eyes narrowed against the wind and cold, watching the impact zone as one wave after another detonated.

Finally Frosty saw Jay, pointing at a dark spot out among the waves. "There. There he is."

Glancing at his watch, Jeff shook his head in disbelief.

Breaching the storm surf, Jay gulped in a lungful of air before another wave loomed over him. It unloaded atop him with thundering force, driving him down, down, down.

The men on the shore all winced as they witnessed the mauling.

"He can take a beating," Dave, the second surfer, said. "But can he surf?"

Frosty smiled reflectively. "Like nothing you've ever seen."

Pulling up the collar of his US Air Force Reserve jacket to block the wind, Dave said, "Yeah, well, he's still just a kid."

"Kid or not, you know anyone who can tread water in conditions like that for twenty-five minutes without drowning?" Frosty insisted, determined to get all three of his friends on Jay's side.

Tom, the third surfer, said, "You've got a point."

"I'll take that as two yeses." Frosty glanced over to the first man, who kept his eyes on Jay.

"Just make sure he doesn't drop in on me," Jeff said finally.

Frosty grinned like a proud father at his friend's tacit agreement. He wasn't going to let the kid take a shot at Mavericks without its most seasoned surfers' approval. Now that he had it, he was one step closer to finally giving the boy his chance.

That night, Frosty pulled straight into his driveway, without waiting down the street for the lights to go out, like he usually did. Although the second bedroom light was still on, he walked in, anyway, carrying a paper bag. It had finally hit him that if he could feel like a father to Jay, he could surely handle being a father to his own kids, too.

He found Brenda doing the dishes in the new kitchen, up to her elbows in suds. "You're early."

He leaned in to give her a kiss. "Yeah, wanted to get home. Where's Roque?"

"In her room." She looked at him curiously.

"Whatcha got there?"

Opening the paper bag, he pulled out a stack of books. "My, ah . . . my old man used to read these to me when I was a kid. Thought maybe I could start reading to Roque every night. You know, if you think it's something she might like."

This was one of the sweet childhood memories he had tried to suppress, not wanting to dwell on what he had lost, what he would never have again. But he remembered so clearly how his father would tuck him in every night before sitting on the edge of his bed, reading him a chapter each night. They had been halfway through *20,000 Leagues Under the Sea* when his father passed. That was one he might not be able to handle reading to Roque—but maybe he could try. Looking at his wife hopefully, he saw the tears begin to well in her eyes.

But she just nodded and said, "I think she'd like that very much."

"Good. We'll start tonight, then." He picked out two books, *Robinson Crusoe* and *Treasure Island,* figuring he should let his daughter decide which to read first. Hiding a smile, he didn't comment when he saw Brenda wipe a tear away. Then he headed down the hall, happy to be making his wife happy, eager to start doing better for his family.

In the gathering dusk, Frosty stood on the shore with his surfboard as Jay rode in on the last remnants of a wave. "Thought you might be staying out there all night."

Stepping out of the surf, Jay replied, "Probably could, water's so warm."

"Strange, right?" As they headed down the beach, sticking close to the waterline, Frosty explained, "Means the tropical hurricanes from Japan are making their way across the Pacific. Only happens every seven to ten years." He stared out to sea as though watching phantom waves that only he could see. "Last El Niño was '83—brought waves into Mavericks the size of five-story buildings."

Despite the massive waves he had already seen at Mavericks, Jay couldn't even imagine a wave of that magnitude. Following Frosty's gaze, Jay felt a shiver go up his spine at the thought of facing such a monster. "And you think El Niño might happen again this year?"

"Don't know," Frosty said with a shrug, "but if it does, you'd better be ready. 'Cuz that wave of ours is not gonna remain a secret."

Jay couldn't believe his training might be almost over, that the day when he would take on his own giant wave was now looming on the horizon. It felt like he had been dreaming of Mavericks forever, and yet he wasn't sure he was ready. He guessed he would never know till he tried.

CHAPTER 18

◀ ▶

Hair still wet, Jay pulled on a T-shirt as he exited the steamy bathroom. As he passed, he glanced into his mom's room, and was surprised to see that her bed was empty. "Mom?" he called.

As he grabbed a banana from the kitchen counter, he saw Christy through the window, driving off in her station wagon. Checking his watch, he had to smile. Unbelievably, she was actually leaving on time, without any help from him.

After he finished the banana, he darted into the back unit to grab some lunch money. Opening his cigar box, he found it empty, except for the unopened letter from his father. Furious, he hurled the box across the room and stormed out. Here he had thought, for just one second, that his mom was doing better, that she was becoming an actual grown-up. But of course that was stupid. She couldn't handle *anything*, couldn't be trusted, just did what she wanted, took like she wanted, exactly like a selfish child. He skated fast and hard to school, his anger propelling him through the streets. Although he considered ditching school, heading out to Pleasure Point Ravine or Pillar Point again, he knew he had missed too many days already, and made himself go. At least he knew what it meant to follow through on his responsibilities.

His fury followed him through the school day. After all the money he had given his mom, how hard he had worked to help support her, he couldn't believe she would just *steal* from him. Even though he needed that money, he would have given it to her, every penny, if only she had asked. His classes passed in a blur. He couldn't focus on anything any of his teachers said, which probably meant he might as well have skipped, but at least it wasn't another absence on the books. They didn't have to know he wasn't really there. The only thing that got him through the day was the hope of seeing Kim after school. She always made him feel better.

But as he waited beside her Jeep that afternoon, clutching his skateboard to his chest, he started to feel awkward. They were friends, sure, but they didn't usually talk at school. Shifting from one foot to the other, he scanned the crowd for her, hoping she would show up soon, before he lost his nerve. His hands started to sweat, and he wiped them off on his jeans. He finally spotted Kim among the students that flooded out of the school, heading down a shaded walkway with her friends. They made eye contact for a moment, but as he started to wave, she turned back to her conversation.

Feeling foolish for having expected anything else, he skated away as fast as he could go. Of course their night at the ravine hadn't meant as much to her as it had to him. Why would it? She was his dream girl, and he was just a kid she sometimes hung out with. Besides, there was nothing she could say that would make him feel better about his mom's betrayal. And how could he admit to her that his mom had stolen from him? It wasn't like he needed her thinking he was trashier than she probably already did. Waiting for her had been a dumb idea, all around. He really should have known better.

What he didn't see as he fled was Kim saying good-bye to her friends and heading toward him, only to find him already gone.

Jay raced to the abandoned house where he and his friends liked to skateboard, ducking through the fence to find Blond and Bells huddled in the shallow end of the drained pool. As he approached, Jay sniffed the air. "Guys, smell that? Something's burning."

Bells whirled to face him. "Past tense, bro," he replied with a glassy-eyed smirk.

"Where there's smoke, there's fire," a taunting voice said. Whipping around, Jay saw that it was Sonny who had spoken. He and his crew slouched, shirtless, around a broken-down wooden table, their skateboards leaning against the garage.

Jay's gaze shot over to Blond. "What're they doing here?" This was a spot he and Blond had discovered together. Bells was the only other person they had ever brought here.

"What, you part of neighborhood watch now?" Blond demanded.

"We came to see the Mavericks Man," Sonny said, his voice a singsong.

Jay's stomach tightened into a knot. First, he couldn't believe Blond had read his notebook.

But more than that, he couldn't believe his friend had told these punks about Mavericks.

"So, you gonna slay that dragon all by yourself, Little Trash?" Sonny stood, kicking the wobbly plastic chair over behind him. Advancing on Jay, he taunted him, "Or that rent-a-dad of yours gonna help?"

"Ol' Frosty the Snowman," said one of his friends, snickering. The others all laughed, an easy audience, united in their derision toward Jay.

"You're higher than us, you think that wave's real," another of the punks added.

"Whole fairy tale's fascinating, though. The warrior's training, the mentor, even the fair maiden." Sneering, Sonny pulled Jay's notebook from beneath his board and began to read. "'From a distance, I watched and realized that along with rare beauty comes constant scrutiny, like being the lead in a school play.'" Staring at Jay, he said with mock sincerity, "That's really poetic, man." Sonny tossed the notebook at Jay, and it landed in the dirt at his feet.

Jay turned away, anguished at having his most private thoughts and dreams laid bare to this thug. He stared daggers at Blond, who laughed along with the rest of them. His friend's betrayal cut Jay as deep as his mom's had.

"Shame she laughs at you behind your back," Sonny continued. Jay struggled to keep the pain from his face, but could feel himself failing. "But, wait, you knew that, right? I mean, kinda obvious since she won't be seen with you."

Although he felt like his heart was collapsing, Jay picked up his notebook from the ground, willing his legs to carry him back across the yard. As he climbed back over the fence, he heard Sonny shouting after him, "Paddle, paddle, paddle, little grom!"

Skating as fast as he could, Jay tried not to think. He sprinted across his yard and threw open the door to his place. He yanked on his wetsuit, hoisted his board, and marched toward the Pleasure Point Ravine.

His feet pounded down the rocky riverbed, and he only paused in his furious motion once he reached the sand. Kneeling, he began waxing down his board. Anger contorted his face as he fiercely rubbed the wax into the deck in a constant, frantic motion, as though trying to wipe out the pain. There was nothing to hold on to. The unending loop of this horrible day spooled out in his mind: His mother had taken advantage of him; the girl he loved had ignored him; his friends had stabbed him in the back. All he had left was surfing, so that was what he intended to do.

After a few hours on the waves, he felt himself growing calmer. The anger wasn't gone, but it was dampened somewhat by giving himself over to the constant ebb and flow of the sea. But he didn't know how he would ever go home. How could he ever stand to face his mom? Sure, he could hide out in the back unit most of the time, but he would have to talk to her again eventually, and he couldn't imagine that conversation going well. He didn't know how he would stand going to school, either. He couldn't handle the thought of seeing Kim, or Blond. At least Bells never went to school, so Jay didn't have to worry about him.

Finally, he was exhausted enough to go home. Although he wanted to go straight to his room to make sure he wouldn't run into his mom, he was starving. He stopped by the kitchen, grabbing a bag of chips out of the pantry. Standing there dripping on the linoleum in the dark kitchen, he shoved handfuls of chips into his mouth, crunching them into oblivion. As he turned to leave, he found a letter addressed to him on the table, and ripped it open. It was the essay on fear he had written for Frosty, with the words "DO OVER!" scribbled across the top. After all the work he had put into it, after everything he had given up for just a shot at riding Mavericks, something snapped inside him when he saw those words.

He stormed out of the house, slamming the door behind him, and ran straight to Frosty's surf shed. Knocking hard on the door, he didn't wait for an answer before yanking it open. Inside, Frosty worked beneath a dim light, glassing in a fin on a long board.

"Evening," he said, glancing over his shoulder at Jay before returning to his work.

"Just wanted to bring this back." Jay tossed the essay down beside Frosty. "Rewritten it twice already. I'm not doing it again."

Without looking up, Frosty continued meticulously aligning the fin. "Up to you."

But as Jay headed for the door, Frosty added, "Deal was: no questions, no arguing, end of story. You wanna walk, that's your choice."

Jay stopped, swallowing back the pain. He had worked so hard, had done everything Frosty asked, and still, it wasn't enough. It seemed like nothing he did was ever enough. Turning to face his mentor, he whispered, "Why're you doing this to me?"

For the first time since Jay had burst into the shed, Frosty met his eyes. "'Cuz I want the truth. For you, not me. So what's it gonna be?"

"I don't know." The words were barely audible.

"You don't know, or you don't wanna know?"

"I don't know!" Jay screamed, hurt and frustration and anger all bursting out in those few words.

"Well, you get one shot, so you better figure it out." Setting aside the board, Frosty stood up, suddenly looming over Jay. "And ask yourself: What am I gonna leave behind? The truth of who I really was? Or just a bunch of words on a page. All that stuff burning deep down in you, stuff you can't even look at 'cuz it scares you so much. What is that, huh? Is it the same thing that's in that letter you can't open but never throw away?"

"Don't do this," Jay begged. He couldn't stand losing Frosty, too, not after everything this day had already taken from him.

"Do what? 'Cuz if you don't wanna go there, if you don't have the courage to open that letter, then how can you possibly take on that wave?"

"Stop it!" Jay cried. "I don't know, all right?"

"Like I said, your choice." Frosty sat back down in his recliner and turned back to his board, the conversation clearly over.

But before Jay could manage an answer, the door banged open to reveal Roque, eyes wide with panic.

"Dadda, quick! Mommy's sick!" she cried.

In a flash, Frosty pushed past Jay and out the door. He bolted into the kitchen, Jay and Roque trailing behind him. He found Brenda kneeling on the floor, head down with one hand braced against the butcher-block counter.

"Bren?" As he rushed over, she collapsed onto the tiles. Frosty rolled her into his arms, pushing her long brown hair back from her face so he could look at her. The entire left side of her face was slack, giving it the appearance of melted candle wax.

Roque recoiled, horrified. "Mommy?"

Her voice badly slurred, Brenda said, "'S all right, baby. 'S all right . . ."

"She's having a stroke," Frosty shouted. "Jay, call nine-one-one!"

Jay ran for the phone as Roque began to cry.

While Frosty cradled Brenda in helpless shock, rocking her in his arms, Jay tried frantically to explain to the dispatcher what had happened, though he didn't understand it himself.

CHAPTER 19

◀ ▶

In his black suit, Frosty stood behind the safety rail at Steamer Lane, his red gun leaning beside him. With a burst of energy, he hurled his board into the waves below, staring down at the pounding shore break as it shattered the gun against the sharp rocks. He wouldn't need it anymore. He was never going to ride a monster wave again. Even though he hadn't kept his promise to stop surfing Mavericks when Brenda was alive, he was going to keep it now, now that he was all his kids had left. Within moments, the shore was covered in a wash of red flotsam, like the shards of his broken heart.

Across the street, the church parking lot was half filled with the cars of friends and family who had come to pay their respects. It had been packed earlier—everyone knew Brenda around here, and everyone loved her—but most of them had cleared out already.

Dressed in an ill-fitting black sport coat and ineptly knotted tie, Jay tentatively approached. But as he drew near, Frosty whispered bitterly, "Go away."

Before Jay could make an escape, Brenda's father crossed the street to join them. "My grandchildren are wondering where their father is," the formidable man said in his thick Southern accent.

Frosty didn't take his eyes from the ocean. "No. They're wondering where their mother is. Sir."

"Then tell them." His father-in-law's voice was firm, commanding.

Gripping the railing, Frosty replied, "I don't know what to say."

"Tell them the truth. Tell them she's in heaven. At the side of God."

"Not sure what I believe right now." Of course he wanted to picture his wife sitting on a cloud, strumming a harp with the angels, but he just couldn't.

"Then you'd better find it quick. You wanted

to cast my daughter's ashes into your beloved ocean, like fish food. Maybe that would've been more 'spiritual' for you? They throw that word around a lot out here." The man stood up straight, pinioning Frosty with his glare.

Jay stood paralyzed beside Frosty, barely breathing. Frosty wanted to tell the kid to flee while he could, but he couldn't speak.

"I'll tell you what. We'll take the kids for a couple of days. But those two children have already lost their mother. Don't rob them of God's comfort, too. Now come inside." Grasping Frosty's arm, he tried to guide his son-in-law away from the railing.

But Frosty was too broken to do what he knew he should. "I can't," he murmured.

He could feel his father-in-law's disappointment emanating off him as he turned and walked back to the church. Frosty watched him go, the man's broad shoulders stooped with the weight of his loss, while he and Jay both remained frozen at the edge of the abyss.

Late that night, Jay sat on the track platform at the peak of the Giant Dipper on the boardwalk. His legs dangled over the side, five stories above the abandoned boardwalk, the wooden roller coaster looming against the stormy sky like a sleeping dinosaur. Below, an ocean breeze whipped across the beach, scattering paper cups and sandwich wrappers. The wind blew across Jay's solemn face, his world shattered. Staring out to sea, he watched the storm clouds gather on the dark horizon.

Noticing a flash of light, Jay looked down to see the outline of an old security guard, aiming his flashlight up at him. "Hey! Hey you!" the man shouted. "What do you think you're doing?"

Jay stared down at the man for a long moment before murmuring, "Just needed to *feel* it." And then he began the long climb down. With the security guard watching his every move, he spoke louder. "Sorry, sorry, won't happen again."

When his feet touched the wooden planks of the boardwalk, the guard nodded. "All right. See that it doesn't."

He biked slowly home through the stormy dark, missing Brenda, who had become like a mother to him these past few months—or at least, like the mother he wished he had. At the same time, he still felt sorry for himself, for all the other horrible things that had happened to him these past few days, and felt awful about it in the face of Frosty and the kids' much greater loss. And yet, his own losses kept mounting: his father, his trust in his mother, Kim, his friends, Brenda, Frosty. He couldn't understand why nothing seemed to last.

When he reached his bungalow, he slipped inside, feeling his way through the darkness to his mom's room. He watched her sleeping, then crept into the room, lying down atop her pink comforter beside her. Despite what she had done, she was still his mom, and he didn't know where else to go for comfort. After staring up at the motionless ceiling fan for what felt like forever, he whispered, "Why did he leave us?"

His mom rolled over, wide-awake, and gazed at him sadly. "He didn't leave *us*, Jay. He left *me*." It occurred to him that she had been lying awake the whole time, just waiting for him to speak. Wiping away her own tears, Christy reached out and gently touched Jay's face.

He wasn't sure the distinction mattered. After all, you could end a marriage without abandoning your kid. He knew his mom wasn't easy to live with—he'd struggled a lot with her issues over the year, for sure—but it hit him that he had been blaming her for driving his father away. Whatever had happened between them, his father could have chosen to do things differently, could have chosen to stay in his son's life, but he hadn't. It wasn't fair, he thought, to punish the one who had stayed.

With that realization washing over him, he allowed his mom to pull him into a hug, dozing off snuggled up to his mom like a little kid after a nightmare.

In the morning, Jay knocked on Frosty's front door, holding a take-out bag full of breakfast food from a local diner. It wouldn't be as good as Brenda's, but he figured Frosty had to eat something. Although Frosty's van was in the driveway, no one answered the door. Looking toward the shed, Jay called, "Frost, you here?"

There was no reply. He tried the doorknob and found it unlocked. Walking into the kitchen, Jay was shocked to see that it had been ripped apart. Everything they had so carefully built for Brenda had been smashed and shredded, the cyclone of Frosty's rage and grief made obvious by the sledgehammer still wedged into one of the cabinets.

The tiles were broken, the cabinets torn down, the countertop chopped to pieces like so much firewood. Jay couldn't believe it and yet, he could understand how pain could drive you to destruction. But now he was really worried. Noticing that the back door was ajar, Jay headed for it. As he stepped outside, he heard the unmistakable sound of Brenda's voice emanating from the surf shed.

"Say hi, Dadda! Say hi!" she called, giggling.

Following the voice, Jay slipped inside the shed to find a video playing on Frosty's little TV. As Brenda waved fourteen-month-old Roque's hand at the camera, Frosty's voice came from off-screen. "Hey there, little pumpkin."

Baby Roque squealed, "Dadda . . . Dadda!" in response.

Jay's heart clenched at the sight of this perfect family scene, now lost forever. As he looked around for Frosty, he noticed the man's water bottle lying on the floor. Glancing up, he saw that the red paddleboard was missing from the rafters overhead. He knew immediately where Frosty had gone.

As he knee paddled through the mystical heat vapors on Monterey Bay, Jay kept his eyes focused on the compass on the front of the paddleboard. Strokes fast and breath steady, he paddled hard out onto the water. Nearing the middle of the bay, he began to feel how alone he was, and fought back the fear by repeating Frosty's words to himself, "Deep breaths, steady rhythm, drive and glide . . . drive and glide."

A pelican swooped down like a demon, gliding past him only a foot above the ocean's surface. The sun bore down on him as if he were a bug beneath a magnifying glass, its intensity exponential as it reflected off the water. Looking around, he took in the breadth of the ocean that surrounded him, a vast universe of incessantly moving water.

Paddling ever faster, his fatigue began to set in. He ripped the cap off his water bottle and accidentally dropped the lid into the ocean in his eagerness to get it open, pouring the water down his throat as fast as he could. Arching his back to relieve the ache from leaning over the board for so long, he screamed into the abyss. "Frosty! Frosty!"

When his shouts faded almost immediately into silence, he felt his panic building. Jay summoned his inner calm, trying to remember what Frosty had told him about the times when he had gone out on the bay. "You paddled to the deepest part. Just to feel it," he whispered to himself. "And you, what?"

Staring at the water for inspiration, he saw the nearly imperceptible current begin to carry his water bottle's cap away. "The current. You drifted with the current." Spinning his board toward the current, he dug in deep again.

Squinting toward the bright horizon, Jay saw the Monterey Peninsula looming like a mirage. In the glare, he made out something else: an outline of a board floating a couple of hundred yards away. With a burst of strength, Jay paddled at a frenzied pace.

"Frosty! Frosty!" he screamed, his emotion building with each stroke.

As he drew closer, he made out the older surfer lying supine on his board. Finally he reached Frosty, his eyes half open, arms trailing in the water. Jay made a beeline for him, his anger welling up, edging out the fear. "Frosty!"

The older man blinked at him, uncomprehending. As he started to sit up, Jay's board collided with his, nearly knocking the man into the ocean.

An unbounded fury erupted from Jay as he

launched himself at Frosty. "What're you doing?" he demanded.

Fighting for balance as he sat up, Frosty attempted to push Jay away. But Jay wouldn't stop, relentlessly shoving him in the chest, each blow fueled by years of pent-up rage. "You can't do this and walk away from everything!"

Seizing Jay's wrists, Frosty demanded, "And why not?"

Clenching his jaw, Jay fought back with every fiber of his being, locked in an adrenaline-fueled struggle with the man he respected most in the world. But finally he pushed past the pain to manage the words, "Because I won't let you." Once the words were out, the tears flowed freely.

Frosty released him, his face registering shame at the hurt he had caused. "You and me was all Brenda's idea, not mine."

"I don't believe you," Jay said quietly.

"We're not that almighty and all-powerful, thinking we can rescue something when we can't even take care of ourselves."

At first Jay didn't know what to say, but then the words came to him—Frosty's words. "Like you said, if you look hard enough, there's always a way through it."

"And what if I don't have the strength?" Frosty looked so lost, like a little boy, that Jay suddenly found strength that he hadn't known he had.

As the two locked eyes, Jay wiped the tears from his face. "Then lean on the fifth pillar."

"Which is what?"

"Me." He no longer felt like an indebted child. Sure, Frosty had helped him, but he knew now that he could help Frosty, too. Maybe that was why Brenda had brought them together—maybe she had known, somehow, that they were going to need each other. For the first time, he felt that they were equals, a team. "C'mon, enough of this. Time to go." He spoke with a self-assurance he had never felt with his mentor before. "Drive and glide."

"Headed the wrong way, chief," Frosty told him as Jay set off.

Eyes still shining with confidence, Jay replied, "I felt the back eddy, Frost. We're more than halfway across the bay. Closer to what's in front of us than behind. C'mon, paddle."

Despite his obvious exhaustion, Frosty had to smile as they began paddling toward the shore of Monterey.

When they reached the coastline, they dragged

their paddleboards high up onto the rocky shoals below Cannery Row. Jay glanced up at the rows of stores and restaurants that lined the pier, happy-looking people strolling along the wide sidewalks. It was a beautiful spot, so close to home and yet so different. As he and Frosty sat atop the breakwater, staring out at the bloodred afterglow of the sunset, neither of them spoke a word. The sound of jazz floated from one of the restaurants, and that mingled with the crash of the waves, those sounds filling the air instead. They stayed there for a long time, exhaustion combined with a sense of accomplishment keeping them both happily immobile as the darkness fell.

CHAPTER 20

◀ ▶

Sun-scorched and stiff from his ride across the bay, Jay stumbled into his kitchen the next morning to find Christy making breakfast.

"You want cheese in your eggs?" she asked, looking up at him.

"Sure." He was too tired to even comment on how strange it was that she was cooking. Noticing a gift-wrapped package on the counter, he raised his eyebrows.

"You forget what day it is?" She smiled, and he shook his head. Of course he knew it was his sixteenth birthday. He just hadn't actually expected anyone else to remember.

Rubbing his eyes, Jay climbed up on the barstool at the counter and tore off the wrapping paper. Inside, he found a Radio Shack weather radio—the one from the ad he had kept all this time. His face registered utter surprise.

Grinning, his mom placed an envelope on the counter in front of him. "And here's all the money I borrowed from you. With a little interest. Sorry about that, baby. Never should've taken it without asking you. Was a little short on the rent, and well . . . freaked out a little."

"But where did—" he began, confused.

"They made me shift manager. Because I'm so 'punctual.'" They shared a laugh at that, both aware that without Jay's help, she was anything but. "I'll make enough now not to have to rent out that back unit anymore, okay? You don't have to worry about that again. Maybe you could even cut back on your shifts at Pleasure Pizza, whaddya think?"

He shook his head, a lump rising in his throat that made it hard to talk. After everything they had been through, she was finally getting things together. Still, he didn't want to assume that everything was going to magically be okay now. Chances were, they would still need his income— and he didn't mind that so much. "Nah. Wouldn't know what to do with all that free time."

Nodding at the shortwave, she said, "Frosty

said you'd be needing that to follow the swells. Said there were gonna be some big ones coming, something about low and high pressure. I didn't understand a lick, but they're calling it 'El Niño.' Which means 'the boy,' as you probably know from getting a C in Spanish."

Jay eyed her in astonishment as she slid his bacon and eggs onto a plate. "You mean . . . you knew all along?"

"Frosty's no dummy. Besides, my handwriting ain't that good. He told me what you were doing, and how much it meant to you. So I said okay."

Springing from his chair, Jay wrapped his arms around Christy, hugging her so hard that he lifted her off the ground. Now he felt bad for keeping it from her, thinking she wouldn't support him or understand. Here he had assumed she wasn't paying attention, when she actually knew everything about him, and accepted all of it.

"Happy birthday, baby," she whispered into his hair. "Just promise me you'll be careful. You're my whole world, you know."

Honestly, he hadn't thought of that. He knew she needed him, but he hadn't realized how much she cared. His arms wrapped tight around her, he felt like he finally had a mother again.

• • •

It was pouring as Frosty and Jay got out of the van at the Pearson Arrow warehouse. Covering their heads, they sprinted inside.

The owner of the surfboard company met them at the door, covered in a fine white dust. "Nice weather we're having, eh, ladies?" He clapped Frosty on the back with the easy camaraderie of old friends. Turning to Jay, he shook his hand. "Bob Pearson. You must be Jay Moriarity. Heard a lot about you, kid. Follow me."

Jay couldn't manage a response, he was so starstruck at having just met one of the best surfboard makers in the world. And knowing that Frosty had told this surfing legend about him was quite simply mind-boggling.

With Bob leading the way through the cavernous warehouse, Jay gazed at the collection of surfboards gleaming like giant sticks of candy all along the walls. Being in this place was like a dream come true.

They passed resin-stained cubicles where shapers were busy sanding and glassing, surgical masks affixed to their intent faces. Bob led them past his cluttered office, walls plastered with surf photos ripped from the pages of *Surfer* magazine.

A TV set blared on his desk. "Evacuations are underway as this punishing storm known as El Niño continues to attack the entire Northwest coastline—" the newscaster announced.

Jay slowed to take in the news footage, watching mammoth waves erupting atop the breakwaters, boats capsized in the nearby harbor, stormy shore breaks crashing through beachfront homes.

Hurrying to catch up with the two men, Jay couldn't stop thinking about something Frosty had told him, another thing he had jotted down in his notebook: *"Waves are the offspring of storms, forwarded by the tiniest of molecules, each affecting the next. Their journey's short, their impact immense, delivered in a form as perfect as it is fleeting."* A storm like that meant killer waves. He just hoped that Frosty would deem him ready in time to catch them.

When they reached Bob's private shaping room, the man said, "You wanna slay a giant, you're gonna need a sacred spear." Flipping on the light, he revealed a gleaming, multicolored gun sitting on a sawhorse.

"Happy birthday, chief," Frosty said.

Jay's jaw dropped. Speechless, he approached

the board, running his fingers along the polished rails as he slowly circled it. It shone in shades of red, orange, yellow, and green. It was, without a doubt, the most beautiful board he had ever seen.

"It's ten-foot-two, nineteen and three-quarter inches wide," Bob explained. "Adjusted the rake to reduce the drag, and increased the tail kick."

"So the board'll turn tighter, quicker," Frosty added.

"But most important, I lowered the nose rocker a half inch." Bob pointed out each feature as he spoke.

"And that's gonna help you get into the wave," Frosty chimed in. "There's an enemy out there you're not gonna see, Jay, and that's the wind." As Frosty lectured, Bob nodded his agreement. "This wave is so huge that when it pitches, it's gonna suck all that offshore wind and force it right up the face. You don't make the takeoff in that split second? That wind'll blast you off the lip and into the air like a kite into space. And trust me, that's a place you do not want to be."

Jay swallowed hard at Frosty's words. Taking on this wave wasn't about thrills—it was a life-or-death proposition, the classic struggle of man versus nature. He was doing it because it was something he felt he *had* to do, but Frosty's warning almost made him wish he could be happy conquering fifteen-footers like he used to do. But his training had shown him that he was a big-wave surfer, through and through, and nothing was going to turn him away from his destiny.

"As far as the color, you gotta ask the scholar here, 'cuz it's all Greek to me," Bob said, interrupting Jay's thoughts.

"The ancient Greeks thought the messengers to the gods traveled via the rainbow at the speed of light," Frosty told him. "Light as you are, you'll need all the speed you can muster out there. The colors are simply to remind you of that."

"I . . . I don't know what to say." Jay's eyes were bright with joy as he looked from the board to Frosty and back again. He couldn't think of a way to thank the man for this present—it was the best thing anyone had ever given him, the absolute perfect gift.

"Just promise to stay low and go fast," Frosty said gruffly.

Jay nodded. Bob pulled Frosty aside as Jay continued admiring the board.

"He has no idea what he's getting into, does he?" Bob whispered.

"How could he?" Frosty just shook his head. Jay pretended not to hear. After all, with a board like this, what did he have to fear?

That evening, Jay ran along West Cliff Road in the rain, water peppering his face, veins bulging in his neck as he held his breath once more. Checking his wristwatch, he stepped up the pace as if racing time itself, his face turning a deep crimson. When his watch's alarm beeped, Jay stumbled to a stop, gasping for air. Turning it off, he smiled at the final count: 4:07. Frosty had said he needed at least four minutes to survive going under at Mavericks, and now he could do it. He was starting to feel like those monster waves might be within his grasp.

The rain was still pounding down as Jay finished up the dishes in the Pleasure Pizza kitchen that night. Turning off the storefront lights, he listened to the weather report on his new radio. "Buoys reporting twenty-six feet at fifteen seconds with swells northwest at two hundred, eighty-five—" said the NOAA recording. Absorbing the significance of this news, he clicked the radio off just in time to hear a knock at the door. Unlocking the door, he opened it to reveal Kim, draped in a dark raincoat, shivering as the torrents sluiced off her.

"Hey. Come in, you're getting soaked." He motioned her in and shut the door behind them.

Shaking off the rain, she said, "It's coming down in buckets."

An awkward silence hung between them. Leaning against the wall, she twisted at a button on her raincoat. She was the one who had come to see him, but it seemed it was up to him to make conversation. They hadn't spoken since that night at the ravine, not even when he saw her at Brenda's funeral. He hadn't been able to handle the thought of any more heartache on a day like that.

"So . . . how you been?" he asked.

"Good. I mean, okay, I guess. You?"

"Not bad." Eyeing her with concern, he tried to determine whether her cheeks were streaked with rain or tears. "You, um . . . sure you're all right?"

Kim finally met his gaze, eyes brimming with emotion. Shaking her head, she slid down the wall, pulling her knees to her chest. Jay sat down beside her on the linoleum floor, the sound of rain against the windows accentuating the stillness.

Finally, she whispered, "The worst lies, Jay, are the ones we tell ourselves in secret."

"Look, you don't have to explain yourself to me." He wasn't sure he wanted to hear this.

Frustration rising, she tensed beside him. "Yes, I do. Because there's more to it than that, there always has been. These . . . complications."

"Meaning what?" He thought he knew, but he wanted to hear her say it.

"The way I act around you . . . it isn't right. All this flirting when we're alone and ignoring you in front of people." He opened his mouth to protest and she shook her head, stopping him. "No, that's what I do, and I've been telling myself it's no big deal, but it is, Jay, because that's not fair to you. I mean, so what if you're younger than me? In ten years, is that really gonna matter? And my parents, my friends—if they knew you like I do, they'd understand. . . . Everything I've been looking at as a good reason not to . . . well, it's all just so shallow I can't even stand it."

"You're not shallow. Not from where I'm

sitting." He scooted ever so slightly closer to her.

"That's because you only see the good in everything. But most of us don't, Jay." Her voice took on an additional urgency as she tried to make him understand. "Instead we dwell on the what-ifs. Why things won't work or can't ever align. Stars, people, life . . . love. And over time we convince ourselves of that."

"And what if you're wrong?" He met her eyes now, searchingly.

"Then you show up at a pizza parlor, in the rain, late one night." She seemed to be forcing the words out, but she didn't let herself stop. "Because you realize . . . the heart has reasons that reason can't make sense of."

"Like . . . like what?" He thought he had heard that quote before, though he couldn't have said where.

"Ever since we were kids, I had this feeling, deep down inside. This certainty . . . that you were the one, Jay. And that I was gonna spend the rest of my life with you." She reached for him, then drew her hand back, unsure.

Jay forgot to breathe, shaking his head in disbelief.

"What's wrong?" She sounded nervous—as if

there had ever been any chance of him rejecting her.

"Nothing. Just been waiting a long time to hear those words, is all." With that, he leaned in and softly kissed her lips, a moment he had been imagining forever, a moment as perfect in reality as it had been in his dreams.

CHAPTER 21

◀ ▶

Jay rode his bike home along East Cliff Drive through the torrential rain. The pounding surf crashed over the guardrail, flooding the streets as he splashed through the deep puddles.

When he reached the back unit, Jay carefully laid out supplies on his bed: wetsuit, booties, two bars of wax, and a spare leash.

Pacing around the room, he eyed the photos of surfing legends that decorated his walls. There were his heroes: Greg Noll, Randy Rarick, Mark Foo dropping into a wave at Waimea. He paused at this one, reading the quote at the bottom: *"If you want to ride the ultimate wave, you have to be willing to pay the ultimate price."* Realizing the truth of those words, he felt the fear building inside him.

Pacing again, he caught sight of the cigar box sitting on his headboard. He knew Frosty was right that if he was ever going to master his fears, he had to start with that letter. Every fear he had of not being good enough, of being rejected and left alone—all of it stemmed from the day his father had left. He knew that now. Removing the eight-year-old unopened letter, he stared at it for a long moment. Sinking into his chair, he drew in a deep breath and finally ripped into the envelope. He slid out a one-page note, eyes narrowing as he tried to gain some understanding from the few words on the sheet. But there was nothing meaningful there.

He crumpled the page and tossed it aside. After all those years of preserving it, he saw now how worthless it was. Turning instead to his typewriter, he fed in a piece of paper. *"Dear Frosty,"* he typed, face somber as he hammered away at the keys, writing the essay that he hadn't been able to handle writing before.

The sound of an NOAA announcement on his shortwave radio woke Jay from his spot on the lumpy, striped couch. Too wired to sleep, he had come in here to watch TV the night before. He must have eventually passed out on the sofa, still fully dressed.

"December 22, 1994," the voice announced. "Be advised there is an extremely high surf advisory in effect. Buoys reporting thirty-two feet at eighteen seconds with—"

Sitting up, he clicked the radio off. That was all he needed to hear. He stared at the shortwave for a moment, then checked the clock: 3:46 a.m. When the phone rang, Jay jumped to answer it, knowing who it would be.

"Thirty-two at eighteen, yeah, I just heard," he said into the phone. "Okay, I'll call Kim."

When he hung up, he found Christy standing nervously in the kitchen. "Take it today's the day." She looked like she had barely slept, either. He felt bad for waking her, but then realized he couldn't have left to ride those waves without telling her first.

"Sure you don't want to come?" She had said no when he asked the night before, knowing today would probably be the day. But he didn't want to leave her out of his life anymore, not if he could help it.

She shook her head. "You just make sure you come back, you hear?" She hugged Jay, squeezing him close. He understood then, as he felt her heart beating against his own chest, how hard it would be to watch from the shore, helpless, while your only child faced down a monster. Of course she couldn't bear to watch.

Holding Roque by the hand, Frosty carried a sleeping Lake to Zeuf's house.

His neighbor met him at the door. "How big is it?"

Frosty just looked at her, his expression making it clear that the waves were plenty big, no point in quibbling over exact height. She nodded—message received. As he handed the baby to her, she gave his hand a quick squeeze. Snuggling the baby against her, Zeuf leaned down to tousle Roque's long brown hair, earning a sleepy grin from the girl.

Frosty and Roque crossed the street to his van, where Kim was already waiting. Jay dashed over and took shotgun, Roque dozing against Kim's shoulder in the back.

"Sure you got everything?" Frosty asked, glancing at Jay.

Jay nodded. They drove up Highway 1 in anxious silence, staring out at the seemingly infinite waves lining the horizon.

Frosty gestured to a copy of *Surfer* magazine sitting on the dashboard. "'Cuz of that, there'll be a few extra 'cowboys' out there today, trying to prove themselves."

Jay picked up the magazine looking at the grainy shot of Jeff Clark riding a twenty-foot bomb. The caption beneath it read, "The Myth Is Real." This was definitely going to attract a lot of attention. No one outside of Santa Cruz had known about Mavericks before now, and even here, most people didn't believe in it. But there was the monstrous wave, captured in all its glory. Mavericks wasn't a secret anymore.

"A swell with this much west in it means sets'll be shifting, so be prepared," Frosty told him.

His words seemed to finally drive it home to Jay that the moment he had been working toward all this time had arrived. "Can you pull over?" he asked, face going white.

Frosty swerved to the shoulder of the road. The passenger door flew open as soon as he stopped, and Jay vomited onto the ground.

After giving him a moment to collect himself, Frosty resumed the drive to Pillar Point. It wasn't a bad thing for the kid to get those nerves out now. Meant he was taking this as seriously as he should.

As they approached, they saw a giant wave rising taller and taller, propelled by the tumultuous wind, until it collapsed thunderously against the reef. Big enough, indeed.

In the harbor, mastheads creaked with the motion of the swell. Surfers and a lone photographer loaded their gear onto Frank's fishing boat. Frosty recognized the photographer as Bob Barbour, one of the great surfing photographers, with multiple cameras strung around his neck. The man paused to tip his Giants cap to Frosty, and Frosty gave him a nod in return.

Taking in the growing crowd, Frosty told Jay, "This ain't your ordinary day. And the world seems to know it."

Frosty parked next to his three surfing buddies, who were already suiting up. Taking in a few onlookers making their way toward the coastline, Frosty locked somber eyes with them. "End of an innocence, my brothers."

As he slid his rainbow-colored gun out of the rear of the van, Jay saw Blond weaving through the flock of spectators in the parking lot. With his hair sticking up and T-shirt wrinkled, Blond was a mess.

When their eyes met, Blond looked away quickly, and Jay thought his friend wasn't going to speak to him. But then Blond shuffled over, a guilty expression on his face. "Hey."

"Hey." Jay didn't know what to say. He understood that Blond had been hurting, that he was coping with a lot of stuff, too, but sharing Jay's private thoughts and sketches with Sonny— well, that wasn't an easy thing to forgive.

"Coast looks scary, man." It was obvious that Blond felt as awkward as Jay did, and yet he was trying, Jay had to give him that. "Never seen it this big before."

As the waves crashed like dynamite in the distance, Blond stared at his feet, unable to meet Jay's eyes.

Drawing in a deep breath, Jay said, "You know, I been thinking lately, about a lot of things. And you taught me to surf. Never really thanked you for that."

It was true—whatever else had happened between them—he would always be grateful to Blond for reaching out to him on his first day on the waves, for helping him get up that first time.

None of this would have been possible without him. Jay held out his fist, and Blond bumped it with his. Smiling, Jay felt himself filled with a pure rush of forgiveness. So Blond had felt jealous, left out, whatever, and he had made a mistake because of it. Feelings like that could make you do dumb things, Jay knew. But Blond had shown up for him today, on the biggest day of Jay's life, and that was what really mattered.

"I'll be watching you, man," Blond said. He slapped Jay on the back before heading off to find a good vantage point along the railing. After staring after him for a moment, Jay slammed the rear door of the van shut.

Walking over from his truck, Jeff asked, "How you feeling, kid? You ready?" When Jay managed a nod, the man said, "Suit up. We'll paddle out together."

Jay shot Frosty an uncertain glance. "What about you, Frost?"

The surfer shook his head. "Made a promise a while ago, chief." Jay nodded. He knew about Frosty's vow to Brenda.

Jay headed down the path with Frosty's surfing buddies, all carrying their boards. Frosty, Roque, and Kim followed behind.

The boom of the waves against the cliff made the ground vibrate beneath their feet, while the sunlight spread across the early-morning sky. When they reached the end of the path, they saw the monstrous waves, rising to heights of forty feet, lined up as far as the eye could see.

"That ain't El Niño, boys," Dave said. "That's El Jefe, right there."

As she took in Mavericks for the first time, Frosty heard Kim whisper, "You gotta be kidding."

Kim watched intently as Jay zipped up his wetsuit and began waxing down his board. "Jay, this is insane. I mean, look at it out there."

While Jay began gearing up, Jeff pulled Frosty aside. "It's too big for the kid. You know that, don't you?"

Mesmerized by the staggering surf, Frosty simply nodded. But he also knew there would be no stopping Jay from giving it his all.

Jay looked up as the three older surfers headed for the water, then returned to his waxing. Turning to Frosty, Kim gave him a nod, moving aside to give him his turn with Jay.

Crouching down next to Jay, Frosty saw the resolve in the kid's eyes. "I know what you're gonna say, so don't." Jay shook his head. "That wasn't the deal, remember—no questions, no arguing."

Drawing in a shaky breath, Frosty struggled to find the words he needed to say. "I only wanted to tell you something that I should have told you long ago. Which is, it doesn't matter. If you decide to paddle out, or take that drop. What I'm trying to say is . . . I love you no matter what."

He could see Jay fighting as hard as he was himself to contain his emotion. Then the kid steadied himself, pulling an envelope from his backpack and handing it to Frosty. "This is for you."

With that, Jay picked up his board and rushed into the water. Frosty watched him go as Kim came up beside him.

"Why didn't you stop him?" she asked, her anxiety pitching her voice several octaves higher than normal.

"Because it's not possible, sweetheart. You know that. It never was."

As they watched, a thick, dark forty-foot wall of water rose up beneath the first light of the rising sun. The wave exploded with a thunderous roar, only to reveal a bigger wave right behind it.

Once Sonny and a couple of other reckless

surfers jumped off Frank's boat, Frosty counted three boats and fifteen surfers now paddling inside the channel, every one of them in imminent danger. He didn't like it, but all he could do now was believe in his training, and hope Jay would be okay.

"It's shifting! Get back to the channel!" Jeff shouted over the roar of the ocean as Jay paddled closer to him. "Son of a . . . ," he muttered, noticing Jay beside him and giving him a look that was both worried and admiring.

Jay felt completely focused as he approached the other surfers. The fear was gone now, replaced by utter clarity.

"Swing wide! Outside! Outside!" Dave cried.

Jay's heart seemed to jump into his throat as the second wave detonated, sending shock waves through the air and water. Striving for calm, he adjusted his angle toward the channel, sprint paddling past the boats and the inexperienced surfers Frosty had called cowboys.

The third wave reared its massive head, looming high above.

Frosty stood at the northern tip of the bluff beside Bob Pearson, his eyes widened, watching the horizon surge like an army ambush.

"Get outta here! Now!" he heard Frank shout over his radio to the other boat captains.

Bob passed an old pair of army binoculars to Frosty, worry creasing his face. "Somebody's gonna die out there," the man said.

Through the binoculars, Frosty saw his surfing buddies paddling for their lives, up, up, up, and over a massive third wave. But there was no sign of Jay. "C'mon, Jay. Where are you?" he muttered. Frosty panned over to see Frank's boat gunning full throttle for the channel, trying to outrun the cresting wave that loomed over it as if the boat were a toy.

Out of the corner of his eye, he thought he saw something, and panned the binoculars back to find Jay paddling up the face of a forty-foot-plus pitching wave. Jay clawed his way up the vertical wall, penetrating the peak in a rupture of spray before plummeting down the backside, the wave exploding behind him as Jay continued paddling out to sea.

While Frosty watched, two of the random surfers were sucked over the falls, obliterated by the megaton force of nature. Frosty couldn't contain his wry smile. Mavericks was not for the unprepared. The other cowboys were taken out by the crushing spume, as the two remaining boats retreated toward shore, attempting to outrun the avalanche of racing whitewater.

Jay and the three older surfers paddled into the clear as the fourth wave seemed to inhale the entire ocean into itself. His heart pounding, Jay triangulated with the satellite dish on the bluff, tiny spectators arrayed around it. Turning to check for the mushroom-shaped rock, he saw that he was in position. "All right, let's see what you got," he muttered to the wave.

Jay whipped his board around, the leviathan looming over him. Wind howling at his face, he stroked harder as the wave began to pull him up along with it. It rose with the steady inevitability of an elevator: two floors, three, four, until he was staring straight down the face of a five-story black cliff. Immersed in the pure bliss of the moment, Jay gave one last stroke before pushing to his feet. For one perfect moment, he stood at the crest of the wave, arms outstretched, feeling the surge of the ocean beneath his feet.

Suddenly, the offshore wind lifted the nose of his board, levitating him. There was nothing he could do to maintain control. As his board was shot skyward in the blistering wind, he was tossed into the air, plummeting helplessly into the depths, like a human barrel tossed over the edge of Niagara Falls. With a deafening roar, the ten-ton canopy of water exploded atop Jay like a train wreck as he was sucked beneath the sea.

From the bluff, Frosty saw Bob Barbour, still in the fishing boat in the channel, capturing on film both Jay's triumph atop the wave and his dramatic wipeout under it. He didn't want to think that that might be the last photo anyone ever saw of the kid. Of course it was possible to survive a wipeout like that. He had done it himself a time or two. But then again, had those waves really been as massive as this one? Even if they had, he certainly hadn't been a wisp of a sixteen-year-old boy, facing a monster for the very first time. All he could do was hope that his training had somehow given the kid the tools he needed to make it back out again.

Everyone on the cliffs stood riveted as Jay was eclipsed in a frenzy of whitewater and devastation. While the crowd around them gasped and shouted, Kim grabbed on tight to Frosty's arm. As she alternated between hiding her face against his shoulder and staring out to sea in search of Jay, Frosty didn't so much as flinch at her viselike grip. He was frozen by the shock of watching Jay's first monster wave take him out so completely.

Through the binoculars, he saw his friends looking back from the shoulder as another wave broke in the spot where they had last seen Jay. He knew they felt the severity of the situation as strongly as he did. The longer the kid was under, the less likely he was to ever find his way up again. More seasoned surfers than Jay had been destroyed by far lesser waves than that behemoth. There were so many things that could go wrong beneath the ocean. Frosty wasn't one to pray, but in that moment, he wished he was.

Now Frosty and Kim both stared in horror down at the ocean, unable to look away as Jay's board flipped riderless through the spume. Barbour's boat caught up to it and someone pulled the board onto the boat as they searched the waters for Jay. Scanning the churn desperately for some sign of the kid, Frosty felt his fear building, more afraid for the boy than he had ever been for himself. But there was nothing, no sign of him.

Inside the chaotic churn of water, Jay was driven down into the turbulent pit. His limbs felt like they were being ripped from his body as the ocean sucked at him with the power of a turbine engine. He was scared, of course, but he knew he couldn't give in to the fear. Eyes closed, he counted to himself, "One thousand fifteen, one thousand sixteen . . ."

Underwater, the impact of the next wave hit him, like a depth charge taking out a submarine. Blocking out the pain, he kept counting. "One thousand twenty-five, one thousand twenty-six . . ."

Forty feet down, Jay's body was tossed like a rag doll as he continued his seemingly futile fight for the surface. "One thousand forty-three, one thousand forty-four." It suddenly struck him that there might not be a way out of this situation.

Things seemed to be happening in slow motion now, as images from his past flashed through his mind: kissing Kim . . . Frosty's wink and smile . . . hugging his mother on his birthday . . . plummeting down the boardwalk roller coaster. . . . It felt as though he was back on the roller coaster now, whipped around by the surging sea. But the ride ended abruptly as he bounced off the reef bottom, taking the brunt of the impact on his chest. It felt like the whole force of the sea had knocked him against the ocean's floor, and he nearly blacked out from the pain. But through the fog that threatened to overtake him, he heard Frosty's voice in his head. *"Fear's healthy, panic's deadly. You* panic *out there, you* die.*"*

Suppressing the panic and the pain alike, his eyes popped open. He began feeling his way along the reef, pulling himself back to reality, trying to make sense of his surroundings. Gazing up into the dark that stretched far above him, he continued counting, "One thousand fifty-eight . . . one thousand fifty-nine . . ." Blinking in the abyss, he finally made out tiny shafts of sunlight, discernible high above him, and started swimming toward the light.

Now fearing the worst, Frosty and Kim struggled to contain their terror. Frosty could see that the girl was doing everything she could to keep from crying. He wanted to tell her it was okay, this was exactly the right time for her to go ahead and cry, but he couldn't find the right words to bring her comfort instead of despair. It got harder with every second that passed, and Frosty fought back the feeling that he had failed the boy, that all that training hadn't been enough. But suddenly, just short of the rocks, Jay burst out of the whitewater, gasping in lungfuls of air.

"There! There he is! Look!" Kim squealed, jumping up and down and pointing, giddy with relief.

Frosty released a long exhale, as if he had held his breath as long as Jay—maybe he had, he couldn't say for sure. Color slowly returned to his ashen face. Disaster had been averted. His boy was okay.

Amid the whitewater, Jay swam with all his might for the safety of the channel. A boat sped toward him, Barbour leaning over the side to help Jay aboard. Relief washed over him at the realization that he was going to be okay. But as he reached for the photographer's hand, he noticed his rainbow gun lashed to the wheelhouse of the boat. That board was made for one thing, and one thing only: vanquishing monsters. It needed another shot, and so did he. Treading water beside the boat, Jay spoke through heaving breaths. "Toss me . . . my board."

Shocked, Barbour didn't move for a long moment.

"My board, please," Jay insisted.

Barbour stared at him, but a slow understanding dawned across his face. With a nod, he called, "You heard the man," to two bedraggled wannabe surfers, recently fished from the torrid sea. They scrambled to unlash the board and passed it over to Jay. As soon as it was in his hands, Jay launched himself back into the turbulent water and began paddling out again. If he wanted to redeem himself today, there was no time to waste. And no way was he going to let that epic wipeout be the last word on Jay Moriarity at Mavericks.

"Wait a minute," Kim demanded, watching from above. "What's he doing?"

Trying to suppress the pride that swelled within him, bigger than any wave, Frosty said simply, "He came to surf Mavericks."

He could see Kim's shock, her anger even, but he knew for a big-wave surfer like Jay, there was simply no other choice. Of course the kid was giving it another try. That was exactly what he would have done after a wipeout like that. Through the binoculars, Frosty eyed a building wave train on the distant horizon. One of those would be Jay's wave. This time, he was sure, the kid would be ready for whatever it threw at him.

Paddling wide to the outside of the shifting sets, Jay found Sonny sitting in the channel, paralyzed with fear. Jay paddled up right next to him, but Sonny never took his eyes from the apocalyptic surf. Jay sat up silently as a gust of offshore wind swooshed across the surface.

"Swell direction's two eighty-five, which is a lot of west for this place, I guess. And why the sets are shifting." He pointed to the bluff. "See the largest satellite dish up there? If you put yourself at the point of a triangle, between that and that mushroom-shaped rock over there, you'll be all right."

Sonny finally looked at him, as though coming out of a trance. "Who told you all that?"

"Frosty and them." He motioned toward Frosty's friends, pointing out Jeff sitting farthest outside the break. "See that guy sitting on the outside there? Surfed this place all alone for fifteen years before he could convince anyone to paddle out with him. Try to get your head around that one. And those two?" He indicated Dave and Tom. "They were the first ones to try it with him. These guys are giants, you know?" When Sonny still lay frozen on his board, Jay urged, "C'mon, you don't have to surf it, but you came this far. At least you gotta *feel* what it's like out there."

His words finally seemed to pierce through Sonny's hard shell. "Think I've *felt* enough for one day," Sonny said with the barest trace of a smile.

Jay nodded—big-wave surfing wasn't for everyone. But it was the only thing for him. As he turned to paddle toward the wild horizon, he heard Sonny say, "Kill it." Smiling at the encouragement from the guy who had antagonized him for so long, Jay knew anything was possible.

As he took his place beside the three seasoned surfers, Jeff looked over at him with a mixture of admiration and relief. "Glad to see you made it, kid."

Dave's eyes were locked on the looming horizon. "Outside, ladies, and I don't mean maybe." They all paddled toward the emerging mountain of water.

"All right, let's show 'em how we do it," Jeff shouted.

Dave and Tom both spun around on their boards as Jeff and Jay screamed, "Go! Go! Go! Go! Go!"

Reveling in the camaraderie, Jay watched as the two men both kicked through the howling offshore wind and launched themselves from the peak. They air-dropped side by side with mere inches of their tails in contact with the heaving vertical wave before they were able to set a rail.

In that split second, Dave went left and Tom went right, arcing at the speed of downhill racers across the collapsing black mountain of water.

Jay and Jeff cheered wildly for their friends, but the moment was short-lived as they prepared for the next wave.

Though he planned to defer to Jeff, the older man told Jay, "She's all yours, charger."

With that, Jay spun his board around and muttered, "Yee-haw," just as he had heard Frosty do when he rode Mavericks.

Staring over his shoulder at the dark tower of pure perfection, his face lit with utter joy. It was the wave of his dreams.

Paddling hard, Jay rose with the building face of the wave, surrounded by the sound of the wind and the water. His arms windmilled, fighting against the wind as he looked down the vertical precipice. Time ceased to exist as he was overtaken by the feathering peak, gravity forcing him downward as he slid to his feet. His face glowed as he dropped through space, the rush like nothing he had ever felt before. It was everything he had imagined it would be and more.

Watching him take the wave, Kim grasped Frosty's arm tighter than ever.

"Frosty—" she cried, but his eyes never strayed from Jay.

"Shhhhhhhhh," he whispered, silencing her with his resolution.

Tears streamed down his face as he clenched Jay's letter in his hand, its words replaying through his mind.

"Dear Frosty, The truth is, I am afraid. I'm afraid I'll never see my dad again and that my mom will never find happiness. I'm afraid of losing Kim, as she's the love of my life. And of course, I'm afraid of losing you. I'm not sure what you think fathers are supposed to be, but now I know what they should be. I finally read my dad's letter, which was like my last essay to you—just a bunch of words on a page. And it made me realize, that's not what I want to leave behind. I know this sounds strange, but I've always felt I wouldn't be around very long. Like I was just passing through. Which is why I want to take that drop, why I have to make it. Because once I look down over the edge, and I catch it, I'll become part of it. And in that moment, I'll know that I'm alive."

Frosty watched as Jay made the drop and set his rail. With a torque-strained bottom turn, the kid was catapulted down the line, carving the face with a fluid soulfulness beyond his years. The kid was truly a soul surfer.

Beaming down at him, Frosty glowed with the pride of a father. Jay's form was perfect—he had taken in every one of Frosty's lessons and used them to master a skill most surfers could never even approach. But beyond simply managing the wave, Jay had become one with it, an extension of all the power and majesty of the sea. That was the part no one could teach, the part that had to come from within.

Frosty folded the letter along the crease and handed it to Kim with a wink and a smile before lifting Roque onto his shoulders. "You might want that someday," he told Kim.

"Come on, pumpkin," he said to his daughter, "time to go."

Frosty set Roque down by the shoreline before wading out, fully clothed to meet Jay in the shallows. Jay stumbled off his board and into his mentor's bear hug of an embrace as the ocean spray formed a halo around them. Kim had joined Roque on the beach, and the two of them stood smiling in the glow of the two men's joy.

Grinning ear to ear, tears of love and gratitude streamed down Jay's face. For that moment, the rest of the world ceased to exist. It was just the two of them: Man and Boy. Teacher and Student. Father and Son.

EPILOGUE

◀ ▶

2001

The young man continued his descent into the tropical depths. His name had once been Jay Moriarity, but that didn't seem to matter anymore. Here, he was completely at one with the ocean that surrounded him, motionless beneath the sea.

He folded down his index finger, leaving only an outstretched thumb: four minutes and counting. His watch began to beep, but he didn't react, caught up instead in the awe and wonder of his surroundings, a joyous smile brimming across his face.

In the final moment, he thought he saw Frosty and Kim, watching him from the shore. He understood then that they would always be there for him, and he for them, until they were reunited once more. A calm unlike any he had ever known filled him, carrying him away.

The beep of a clock radio's alarm jolted Kim awake in her chair in front of the window. Wrapped in a blanket, she stirred, squinting out the window past the cypress tree to see Frosty leaning against his van. He stared up at her, dressed in a parka with a fullsuit tied at his waist. When he saw her looking, he attempted a smile, but couldn't quite manage it. She understood.

Although she knew she should hurry, she wandered the room, paging through Jay's magical drawings of warriors and waves in his notebook, gazing at the '95 cover of *Surfer* with Jay air-dropping into his first fifty-footer on his rainbow gun, framed on the wall. There were a variety of promotional shots he had taken for his sponsor, O'Neill, so handsome in their gear, so proud to be making his living as a surfer. She stood for a long moment in front of her favorite picture: her and Jay, embracing tightly outside a cheesy white roadside wedding chapel in South Lake Tahoe. Less than a year ago—the happiest day of her life.

She was supposed to be traveling the world with him now. She had been on her way to the airport to meet him in the Maldives, where he had gone on an O'Neill photo shoot, when she got the call.

It was a free-diving accident in the Indian Ocean off the coast of the island Lohifushi. He had been down forty-five feet, meditating on the ocean's floor, the last time anyone saw him. Maybe he got confused on the way back up, or maybe he just held his breath too long—she would never know, exactly. It was incomprehensible, yet if he had to go so soon, she knew he would have wanted it to be the ocean that took him. At least she knew he had been at peace when he passed.

Finally she pulled herself away from the photos, dressing quickly. It seemed impossible that she would ever care what she looked like again, but today was a big day, and she wanted to show the proper reverence. She could barely think the word *widow*, but at twenty-five, that's what she was.

Hurrying downstairs, she hopped in the van, where she and Frosty sat in silence for the drive. The void they were left with was impossible to fill with mere words.

When Frosty parked at Pleasure Point, he and Kim took out their boards. They led a small procession, with Jeff Clark, Dave, Tom, and Bob Pearson following close behind. Turning at a sound behind him, Frosty slowed his gait, face awash in disbelief.

Glancing up, Kim followed his gaze to see a sea of people flowing down the street and bluffs. Friends and neighbors, young and old, an entire community stretching as far as the eye could see. The multitudes parted as they continued down the center of the road, a crowd of kind faces and sorrow-filled smiles, each clutching a surfboard or flowers, many of them with leis draped around their necks—a living, breathing testament to Jay.

Reaching the glassy waters, Frosty and Kim paddled side by side into the ocean, the masses slipping into the sea behind them.

Sitting up on his board, Frosty turned to face the crowd, to say a few words about Jay.

"Jay became famous that first day he surfed Mavericks, not for riding giants, but for the courage of a boy who dared the impossible. Over the years, he rose to the brim of the surfing world, his prowess matched only by his joy, the true prince amid the sport of kings. He married his childhood sweetheart, and swore himself true." He glanced over at Kim, a princess of the sea in her wetsuit and white flower lei, and saw the tears streaking her face. "As for the rest . . . all I will say is, the ones who push the limits sometimes discover . . . the limits sometimes push back." The words caught in his throat, tears blurring his vision, but he was determined to finish.

"We all come from the sea, but we are not all *of* the sea. Those of us who are, we children of the tides, must return to it, again and again, until the day we don't come back, leaving behind only that which was touched along the way." This was the lesson of Jay's life, what he wanted all of these people to take away from this incomparable loss.

Amid the kelp beds, more than a thousand surfers sat atop their boards, fanned out, motionless, around an outrigger. Christy sat in the hull of the canoe next to Zeuf and Melia, who strummed her uke as she softly sang "Kanaka Wai Wai" in her native tongue.

Bobbing atop his board next to Kim and the canoe, Frosty silently mouthed the words of the song, his eyes closed. And then, as though the music was emanating outward from his soul, Frosty began to sing. Melia hesitated, Frosty's words floating just above a whisper, before she began to strum along.

Let me walk through paradise with you
Take my hand and lead me there.

Nearly overcome by emotion, his voice trembled. Kim reached over and took his hand. As if buoyed by her touch, Frosty began to sing louder.

All my early treasures, I would gladly give
Teach me how to love and how to share.

Filling with a glow like the one that had always seemed to emanate from Jay, Frosty felt the mood of the crowd shifting from grief to a celebration of life. That, he knew, was what Jay would have wanted.

Digging deep, feeling himself drawing power from the ocean, Frosty bellowed, "To Jay!" Arms exploding heavenward, he showered water into the air.

From the oceans to the bluffs, a deafening cheer answered him, echoing across the bay. Thousands of arms splashed water into the air, tossing flowers onto the waves, a baptism of petals and sea spray.

At the shore break, a trio of nine-year-old boys brimmed with mischief as they surfed a waist-high wave through the shower of flowers and water droplets, an offshore breeze ruffling the water. Jay was alive in them, Frosty thought—in anyone who took pure joy in surfing, who felt their oneness with the sea.

On their way back up the bluff, Kim spotted Blond, crouched at the crumbling park wall, aerosol can in hand. As he stepped back to examine his work, she saw that he had spray painted over the old graffiti with its petty threats like SURF WHERE YOU LIVE with swirling psychedelic letters that spelled out LIVE . . . LIKE . . . JAY.

She smiled, letting herself be soothed by the outpouring of love, by the sound of the eternal tide gently lapping against the shore below. She and Jay were written in the stars. And their love was eternal, like the ocean, like the stars. She would always love him, and she knew that meant he would never really be very far away.

◀ ▶

Jay Moriarity's spirit lives on in his hometown of Santa Cruz, California; in the nearby coastal areas; and in surfing communities around the world.

Every year, the "Jay Race" paddleboard event takes place in Monterey Bay. The race is twelve miles long, from Capitola to Santa Cruz and back. There is also a novice two-mile race and a race for kids. It's not only a huge family-oriented event, it's also known as one of the biggest and most prestigious paddleboard races in Northern California. Says Kim Moriarity: "The positive vibes and spirit in the air is incredible . . . you can just feel the energy!"

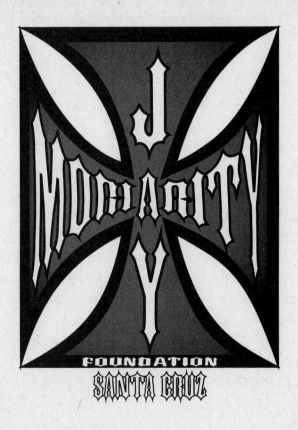

This Iron Cross logo was originally created with Jay's help for his own Pearson Arrow model surfboards. Jay's Iron Cross Model logo lives on through his shaper, Bob Pearson, who continues to shape Jay Moriarity model surfboards, and as the logo of the Jay Moriarity Foundation.

The Jay Moriarity Foundation (http://jaymoriarityfoundation.org/) is a nonprofit organization created in the spirit of Jay to improve the quality of life. The foundation supports existing programs designed to help people and the environment, as well as forming new ways to educate and assist young people along their path.

Says Kim: "In the spirit of Jay, we consider ourselves a 'big bear hug of help' to all that is good." The foundation's motto is "Live like Jay."

[7]